# KEVIN & PERRY GO LARGE

richard topping

based on the screenplay by
harry enfield & david cummings

# B◼XTREE

*For Ian.*
*Best mate.*

First published 2000 by Boxtree
an imprint of Macmillan Publishers Ltd
25 Eccleston Place London SW1W 9NF
Basingstoke and Oxford

www.macmillan.co.uk

Associated companies throughout the world

ISBN 0 7522 7189 X

9 8 7 6 5 4 3 2

A CIP catalogue record for this book is available from the British Library.

Front cover photograph by Stephen Vaughan, © Tiger Aspect Pictures 2000

Designed and typeset by Blackjacks

Printed and bound by Mackays of Chatham plc

# chapter one

The executioner – who, it has to be said, was pretty beefy even by executioner standards – stood on the platform surveying the upturned, expectant faces beneath him. His gaze wandered across the packed castle courtyard and he noted, with grim satisfaction, that it was strangely silent, save the lonely methodical thud of an unseen drum. The air was thick with woodsmoke and the all-pervasive stench of death. Well, it could have been death. Or it might have been the open sewers. Difficult to tell in the middle of the 16th century.

His mind returned to the ominous task ahead, and he gripped his axe just a little harder. This was a good day to die, he thought to himself. Unless you were the one dying, of course. In which case it was probably quite a crappy day to die. Still, not really his problem. He had a job to do, and, let's face it, it's not every day you get to kill a queen. Especially one who was supposed to be as babe-licious as this one.

The doors to the tower on his right swung open and the crowd suddenly erupted into jeers and catcalls. A volley of rotten vegetables flew through the air at the figures emerging from the darkened doorway. The rabble parted to let the procession make its way to the platform, and as the priest and the Lord Chancellor

1

pushed forward he caught his first glimpse of their escort, the Queen Anne Boleyn.

She was — most verily and without a doubt — total top totty.

Young and beautiful, with a long slender neck, delicate face, and quite fantastic-looking boobies, she carefully made her way to the steps of the dais. There she paused and looked up, her eyes meeting those of the executioner. He found her gaze strangely hypnotic — it seemed that, despite her imminent death, she still looked massively up for it. Gagging for it, actually.

She climbed the steps and stood before him, her pierced bellybutton stud glinting in the cold, morning light. With a rather pouty huff she fell to her knees and started to lean across the scarred and bloodstained block. But before she had laid her neck over its terrible grooves, she once again looked upwards into the eyes of the executioner.

'Please don't execute me,' she pleaded, her breasts fetchingly pointy in the cold misty air. 'Tis such a waste of my lovely woman's body. I've got years of shagging left in me. Why chop off my head when thou could lift up my dress and look at my front bottom?'

The executioner — usually implacable in the face of human pleadings — stopped for a moment to consider the options. Great tits. Pointy nips. Available front bottom. Big effort with the axe. Mess to clear up. No shag.

No contest really.

He pulled off his mask, revealing — to a collective sigh from the crowd — the noble and feared face of England's most notorious executioner. Kevin. Or Kevin the Executioner, as he was more commonly known. 'Phwoarrggh! I'm *not* going to kill you...' he said, his face filled with compassion and understanding. The crowd responded with a deafening cheer.

The queen leapt to her feet and kissed Kevin firmly on the mouth, a not-unsaucy kiss that offered the promise of tongue, and more besides. 'Good sir,' she said, her chest heaving, 'I owe thou a shag.'

She fell to her knees and reached for the executioner's flies. The crowd cheered even louder. Those who knew of Kevin the Executioner's fearful reputation held their hands wide above their heads in the universal gesture of 'this big!', and a cry of 'Large!' went around...

'...Kevin. Kevin! KEVIN!'

He awoke from his daydream with a start to see his mother standing in the doorway, her usual look of wary distaste barely concealed. Typical. Abso-bloody-lutely typical. Just about to get a bona fide medieval leg-over and who should go and ruin it all but the old nag herself.

'How's your homework going?' enquired his mother impatiently, trying to pick a path over the detritus that comprised Kevin's room. Her foot narrowly missed a pile of CD cases and found a gap between some discarded magazines and a pile of musty smelling clothing which littered the floor.

'Fine 'til you came in,' snorted Kevin, slumping further down onto the bed and pretending to be riveted by his textbook – The Six Wives of Henry the Eighth – open on his lap. He watched his mother root through his cupboard until she emerged with a plate – or at least something that used to be a plate – covered in a small rainforest of mould and gunk, the crusts of what was once a pizza poking through the foliage. She'd also discovered some mugs which looked similarly botanical, all of which were deposited onto Kevin's desk.

'Can you bring this mess down when you come please?' she said wearily, knowing full well what the response would be.

3

'I am not your slave!' he scoffed.

His dad stuck his head round the door and scowled at him. 'Kevin, don't talk to your mother like that.' They stared at each other until his dad, lacking the energy for an argument, simply withdrew, looking simultaneously furious and confused.

Kevin sneered as they closed the door on him. 'So unfair...' he muttered, suddenly overwhelmed with self-pity and loathing for his life. How could anyone live like this? Persecuted and hounded by his very own parents. Parents who – quite obviously – hated him and wanted him dead.

It was time to commit his thoughts to paper. In years to come these diaries would be pored over by scholars and historians, eager to unravel the intricate and interesting personality of a man who gave so much to the world. A man who rose above the handicaps of a deprived upbringing to become both a pivotal figure of the 21st century, and a notoriously good shag.

He scanned the landfill site of his bedroom and plucked the leather-bound journal from beneath a copy of *Mixmag* and a pair of scuzzy underpants.

'Dear Diary,' he wrote, the weight of history bearing heavy upon his shoulders, 'sorry I've never written in you; I have higher things on my mind. If I did write down my thoughts, you would surely be a worldwide best-seller, for I am truly a genius unrecognized by the world.'

Kevin paused to consider his words – so wise, so illuminating, so important. Already he could picture the scenes of their publication: bookshops besieged by hordes of fans – girls mostly, with exposed midriffs and tanned tummies – clamouring to get a glimpse of him as he signed copy after copy, dispensing wisdom and sex appeal in equal measure. He sighed, and continued writing.

'As yet, the only person who truly understands me

4

is my best mate Perry, who is joyful in his understanding of my bountiful wisdom.' Aah, Perry. No one could ask for a better mate. Until Perry met Kev he was but a humble peasant, but now he was top. Perry, who, if Kevin wore his jacket inside-out as a mark of not conforming to conventional dress patterns, would go one step further and wear his back to front. Perry, who was as completely desperate for a shag as Kevin was. Perry, who knew exactly how important it was to go all the way with a girl before they both died in a horrible accident, which was almost certain to happen because geniuses died early, and Kevin and Perry were, without any doubt whatsoever, teenage prodigies of the first order.

Kevin had read somewhere that true geniuses saw their talent as more of a curse than a gift. Mozart driven to madness by melody. Picasso persecuted by pictures. Kevin haunted by hip-hop. This was a burden he had to carry. No one except Perry understood the affliction of greatness he carried on his shoulders – the responsibility of being possibly the world's greatest living DJ and mixmaster, but forced to hide his brilliance because his parents didn't like loud music. Kevin and Perry's 'Big Girl' mix, for instance, was undoubtedly destined to top the charts and make them trillionaire DJ gods, but every time they rehearsed it, his dad would come into his bedroom and try and unplug the record decks. Such oppression.

Kevin thought this was worth noting, and returned to his diary. 'Although we are currently without a major label contract, we are surely soon to be discovered as the world's top DJ mixmasters. When we are top DJs my parents will surely eat their pants.'

Now, in his vision of the near future, Kevin was signing records instead of books. Everything else was pretty much the same — especially the girls — but this time his parents had to fight their way through the assembled mass to speak to their son, 'You're a genius, darling,' said his mother, in reverent tones. 'You certainly proved us wrong,' said his dad pathetically. And then, from the throng of the crowd, emerged The Supermodel — whose beauteous bikinied form had looked down at him from a poster on the wall — who took Kevin by the hand and led him away for a full-on proper shag.

Once again the monstrous injustice of reality crashed in, and Kevin continued scribbling furiously with renewed angst and misery. 'Dear Diary, like Van Gogh and Kurt Cobain, there is pain behind my genius. For although I've been up for it for almost three whole bloody years, no girl has yet let me go the whole way.'

Kevin, exhausted by this emotional outpouring, put down his pen and looked at what he'd written.

Nothing.

The page was empty, save a single, detailed doodle of a big-breasted woman with very few clothes on. Kevin howled, slammed the diary shut and thundered down the stairs to the front door.

Time to see Perry.

Ernest Buchan looked up from his mowing to see the Patterson boy storm out of the house next door and stomp away up the street, head bowed and hands thrust deep into the pockets of his jacket. The boy's face was thankfully obscured by a hat — the kind Ernest used to wear when he went fishing — but he'd seen it enough times to know what to expect. A permanent acned sulk, usually peering out from beneath an unattractive mop of lank ginger hair. Ernest shuddered. What a nightmare.

He and Mary didn't understand children. Never wanted them, never had them. They were just so... alien. So much unpleasantness. Babies smelled. Toddlers broke things. Kids asked too many questions. Teenagers argued. Students irritated. In fact, there was nothing even remotely redeeming about anyone under the age of twenty-five. Now, if children could emerge as fully formed and functional thirty-year-olds, then Ernest and Mary might have considered parenthood. But since they didn't, he could only look at people like the Pattersons with a sort of bemused pity. Why put yourself through so much misery? They seemed a decent enough couple – he was something in insurance and she did something in an estate agent's, but that boy! As numerous over-heard rows, door slammings, shoutings and stormings-off had testified, he was a walking, talking (grunting, if there was any truth) advert for ever-vigilant birth control. And as for that lumpen twit who seemed to spend his time following one step behind the Patterson boy wherever he went...words failed him.

He shook his head and carried on mowing the lawn. At least with the boy away the whole street wouldn't have to listen to that godawful thumping noise these kids called music.

He glanced at his watch. Soon time for *Antiques Roadshow*.

# chapter two

To passers-by, the two shifty-looking teenagers lurking outside the newsagent's probably looked no different from thousands of other shifty-looking teenagers lurking outside bus-stops, McDonald's restaurants and parks the country over. But if they'd looked a little harder — which of course no one ever does when dealing with the adolescent equivalent of nitro-glycerine — they'd have sensed a more sinister purpose behind the usual aimless loafing.

Kevin and Perry were about to embark on a dangerous mission. Not just any old life-threatening assignment, of course, but *The Big One*. A defining moment of manhood, a rite of passage as old as the lithographic printing press and the invention of the top shelf.

Getting a porno mag.

Kevin had suggested it weeks ago, a plan so ludicrous, so crazy, and so downright dangerous that they just might get away with it. So far, everything was going perfectly according to plan. They'd chosen a newsagent's on the other side of town where no one could possibly recognize them, at a time of the afternoon when the streets were deserted. It was important that there were no witnesses. The thought of actually being seen acquiring a jazz mag was too horrifying to contemplate. Everyone in the world knew what they were for. You might as well just stand in the middle of Trafalgar Square with your trousers round your ankles and a stiffy in your hand. No, this was absolutely the right way to do it. They'd never see the newsagent again and could remain blissfully anonymous for ever.

Kevin made one last scan of the high street and nodded at Perry. 'You got it?' he hissed.

'Yeah,' said Perry, pulling a cosh made from a grubby sports sock stuffed with coins from his pocket.

'I'll get the goods. You give him that.' Kevin nodded at the cosh.

They turned up the collars of their jackets and pulled down their baseball caps until only a sliver of their faces was visible. They looked at each other, took a deep breath, and to Perry's rallying cry of 'Go! Go! Go!' they burst into the newsagent's.

Padwar Patel, father of four and collector of old Doris Day musicals, heard the bell above the door tinkle and looked up from his newspaper to see the two boys skid to a stop. There they began shiftily eyeing up the magazine rack. Padwar knew immediately that they'd come in for one of two reasons. Either to nick sweets, or buy a nudie magazine. Since they looked too old to be out pinching Snickers bars, it had to be the mag. He sighed and turned back to his paper. Same old story.

He'd had this shop for twenty-eight years, and when it came to the top shelf, nothing ever changed. He'd probably dispersed more knowledge about the female anatomy to generations of schoolboys than all the biology teachers in town put together. And it didn't matter if they were seventeen or seventy-seven, they all acted the same way. Edgy and embarrassed. With older lads (and men who should know better), they

9

always bought something else, like *Private Eye* or *Investor's Chronicle*. They'd bring them to the till with the nudie magazine casually tucked beneath the other, as if it was an afterthought. Hey, they were trying to say, I'm an intelligent, cultured sort of bloke who also happens to appreciate artistic photos of ladies with no clothes on. And I'm absolutely not going to dash straight home to the bathroom for a swift twang on the old one-stringed sitar. Really. Who were they trying to kid?

Whilst Padwar ruminated on the purveyors of his best-selling magazines, Kevin was weighing up the relative merits of *XXX Porno Lust Bunnies* versus *Big Bums Bouncy Baps*. It was all a bit tricky, since he was trying to pretend he was looking at the gardening magazines on the shelf below. *XXX Porno Lust Bunnies* seemed the best bet, and responding loyally to an all-familiar stirring in his pants, he lunged for the magazine and grabbed it off the shelf. He shuffled to the till with Perry at his side and in the deepest voice he could muster, said 'This please.'

This was Perry's cue. He whipped the sock out of his pocket and, fumbling madly, scattered the contents of his sister's piggy bank all over the counter, coins bouncing and rolling away in a boisterous clatter. This was all they needed. Kevin and Perry scrambled to pick the pennies off the floor but just when they thought it couldn't get any worse – more disaster. The bell above the door tinkled and they turned round to see a policeman amble into the shop. He moved to the paper rack, and started browsing the headlines on the newspapers.

Perry did not think he had ever, ever been this terrified. He was about to get arrested as a pervert and thrown in jail. His parents would have to watch the trial and he'd probably get shagged in the prison showers by some mass-murdering homosexual. And sex offenders – they got beaten up all the time, didn't they? He'd have to go into a special part of the prison with Ian Brady and the Yorkshire Ripper.

He didn't just have butterflies in his stomach. He had a whole bloody airforce of Harrier Jump Jets and Mig Fighters in vicious air-to-air combat. It was all he could do to stop his legs from buckling beneath him. He was vaguely aware he was hyperventilating.

The shopkeeper, oblivious to the boys' terror, lifted the magazine and tried to read the price on the back cover. Oh dear God, thought Kevin to himself. Please don't let him see. Please, please, please. I'll never buy one ever again. I promise. I promise.

Perry, having just got over the embarrassment of spilling the money everywhere, felt like he was going to throw up. Instead, he did the next worst thing and the dusty calm of the newsagents was disturbed by a long and protracted fart that caught everyone by surprise, not least Perry, who at least had the decency to blush. The shopkeeper looked up, said nothing, and continued his search for the price. Kevin kept glancing back at the policeman who thankfully hadn't heard the commotion in Perry's pants. After an agonizing wait that lasted about eighteen months, the shopkeeper eventually found what he was looking for.

'Three ninety-nine, please,' he said, putting the magazine into a brown paper bag, safe in the knowledge that the lads would only ask for one anyway. Thankful that the wait was finally over, Kevin mumbled a thank you, feverishly grabbed the bag from the shopkeeper's hand and the boys dashed out of the shop.

Mission accomplished.

'You were terrified,' said Kevin as they marched rapidly away down the street, occasionally glancing over their shoulders to make sure they weren't being pursued.

'No I wasn't,' said Perry, who quite clearly was.

'Yes you were. You were scared of the pigs.'

'I ain't scared of the pigs,' said Perry, whose only previous brush with the law was being stopped once because he didn't have any lights on his bike. 'They're scared of me.'

'They're scared of me 'cos I rule this manor,' said Kevin, getting into the swing of things. 'I'm 'ard.'

Perry squeaked, and Kevin turned expecting to see his best friend swaggering along like Grant Mitchell. Instead, Perry stood frozen to the spot, eyes the size of 12-in remixes. 'There's your dad,' said Perry, slack-jawed.

Kevin looked up and sure enough there, not thirty yards down the street, was his dad, strolling towards them and looking aimlessly in the shop windows. *Pants! Pants! Pants!* Kevin emitted a wounded yelp like a rabbit in a snare, and without a second's hesitation thrust the paper bag into Perry's hands, who immediately shoved it back again. In a blur of puffer jacket and brown paper, the mag got thrown back and forth until there was an ominous rip and it flew into the air and landed on the pavement between them, its pages as gloriously open as the girl's legs in the photograph.

The boys looked at each other, their terror complete. In desperation, Kevin did the only honourable thing. He threw himself on the grenade.

Kevin's dad, only a few feet away, looked up just as Kevin hurled himself onto the pavement to cover the magazine. Convinced Kevin was having some kind of seizure, he dropped his briefcase and dashed forward. 'Are you alright, Kevin?' asked Mr Patterson, looking down at his son.

'Oh, hi Dad – yeah, fine thanks.' said Kevin nonchalantly from the ground.

'Why are you lying on the pavement?'

Kevin searched frantically for an excuse that had even the tiniest whiff of believability to it – any excuse – that might get him out of this mess. None came. In the end he said the only thing that came into his head. 'Oh, I'm just a bit tired. I need a sleep.' He yawned theatrically and closed his eyes.

Kevin's dad, now dangerously confused, turned to Perry in the hope of getting some sort of explanation. Perry wasn't much help. He simply got down on the pavement next to Kevin and yawned. 'Yeah, we're knackered, Mr Porn…er Patterson' said Perry, hurriedly trying to cover up his unfortunate slip of the tongue.

Luckily Ray Patterson didn't hear. As he looked down at the two boys in utter disbelief he wondered if – when he was fifteen – he had ever been half the freak that his son seemed to be. He picked up his briefcase and – glancing back over his shoulder – wandered off, his afternoon ruined by thoughts of mental asylums and prescription medication.

Back in Kevin's bedroom, the boys laid on the bed and stared in stunned reverence at the contents of *XXX Porno Lust Bunnies*. It wasn't that they'd never seen a porno mag before, but this was the first one that hadn't been found mouldering in a plastic bag in the park or been handed around the classroom so much that the ink had rubbed off the pages. This was a new porno mag. This was *their* porno mag. This was a very *detailed* porno mag.

They'd gone through the magazine – cover to cover – several times, but there was one particular girl they kept going back to. She was lovely. Beyond lovely, thought Perry, confused as to which bit he ought to be looking at. Her face, her breasts or her…thingy. Was it

13

rude to look at it? She did have it out on show, after all. But she was so pretty it just seemed...not right. Still, she was bloody gorgeous.

'Debbi is from London', read Kevin from the caption accompanying the picture, 'and loves clubbing. "I go to Ibiza every year for the clubs and the carefree sex. It's fantastic. Everyone just gets off with everyone else. It's so horny."'

'I love her, Kev...' said Perry to Kevin, who was staring so hard his eyes had glazed over.

Kevin turned to Perry. He'd just had an idea. A plan so enormously brilliant it solved all of their problems in one fell swoop. Of course! Why hadn't he thought of it before? Maybe he had, but had never given it any *serious* consideration. Yet now, flushed with the success of getting the porno mag and with a stiffy that simply refused to budge, it seemed perfectly feasible.

'Well, that's it!' he said.

'What?' asked Perry, wondering why his best mate had such a weird expression on his face. Actually, Perry didn't want to know. Strange things can happen when you sit reading a porno mag for hours on end whilst having to keep both hands in sight.

'Well, we're DJs – where do DJs go for the summer?' asked Kevin.

Perry's face looked blank. This didn't give Kevin much to go on, since Perry's face nearly always looked blank. Kevin pointed to another magazine on the floor, a copy of *Mixmag* whose front cover was festooned with a banner that read 'Ibiza special'.

Ibiza.

Kevin grinned. 'All girls who go to Ibiza shag anyone, especially DJs. So where are we gonna go?'

Ibiza. *Ibiza!* Sun. Sex. Sand. Sex. Sea. Sex. And Sex.

It was a brilliant plan.

14

*Sullen. Uncommunicative. Lazy.* The words swam out of the pages like bad smells from a dustbin. Mr Patterson couldn't believe it. He knew Kevin's school report wasn't likely to glow, but he had absolutely no idea things had got this bad. The boy's GCSEs were next year, and if things didn't change radically, Kevin was going to be spending even more time in his favourite burger bar – but this time on the other side of the counter wearing a blue uniform.

The afternoon's little scene was just another reminder that the boy was skidding dangerously out of control. What in heaven's name were those two doing *lying on the pavement*? Maybe they were begging for money. Maybe…maybe…there weren't any maybes left. It was all too horrible to contemplate.

He had to find a way to get some leverage on the boy. No threats seemed to work. No punishment seemed to get him motivated. The lad was impossible. You couldn't talk to him – all he did was sulk and walk off, and you certainly couldn't tell him what to do. The only thing he seemed interested in was Perry and those awful record decks he had in his room for doing 'mixes', whatever they were. And any hope of a girlfriend who might calm him down seemed way off the horizon. Kevin was just so gangly and awkward and spotty and…and…he hated to say this about his own son, but in all honesty, he was just so…unattractive. Mr Patterson knew it was a phase all boys went through, growing so quickly over two or three years that their bodies kind of got out of synch. But everything about Kevin seemed more mismatched than most, like a badly constructed skeleton held together by a wet-suit. And the lad didn't do himself any favours with that ridiculously long fringe and the way he moped along with his knuckles dragging on the ground all the time. All in all,

15

Kevin was turning into a problem child, and he seemed powerless to stop it.

He looked up as he heard a familiar thundering down the stairs and Kevin and Perry bounded into the lounge. Either Kevin had forgotten the report was due today, or he'd become so blasé about its contents he didn't do his usual 'skulking around the house in case my dad sees me' routine. Mr Patterson suspected he'd forgotten, a theory instantly proved when Kevin came straight up to him and asked if he could go on holiday to Ibiza – in much the same way you'd ask if you could have another cup of tea or a clean pair of socks.

'Ibiza?' asked Mr Patterson, not quite sure he'd heard correctly.

'Yeah,' replied the boys in unison, all expectant smirks and smiles.

'You think you deserve to go to Ibiza after this?' He held up Kevin's school report like it was a piece of used toilet paper – which in many ways he felt it was. It certainly stunk.

Whoops. Kevin had completely forgotten the reports were sent out yesterday. He should have remembered. Pupils weren't supposed to know the contents before they went in the post, but Kevin had seen his report, from afar, as his form master put it in the envelope. The school had a dumb system where all the teachers wrote good comments in blue, neutral comments in black, and bad comments in red. Even from the very back of the classroom, Kevin could see his report was all red.

'It's even worse than we expected,' said his dad, getting himself well and truly lathered up. '"Kevin lacks application. Is still emerging from an adolescent phase of rebellion which shows no sign of ending." It's just awful isn't it? What have you got to say for yourself?'

Kevin shrugged. In all reality, he didn't have anything to say for himself. School was stupid. His dad was stupid. Reports were stupid. The only things in the world that weren't stupid were Perry and Ibiza. Which – when he thought about it – was the only reason he'd bothered to come downstairs in the first place. 'So can we go to Ibiza?' he asked, convinced his father wouldn't extend this persecution by denying him his right to go on holiday and get shagged.

Mr Patterson couldn't quite believe his eyes. Or his ears. And when Perry stood too close, he couldn't quite believe his nose either. Kevin really thought he was going to be allowed on a holiday, rewarded if you like, for the worst school report ever in the history of bad school reports. The lad's self-delusion was so complete it was almost impressive.

'I think I've answered that question, Kevin. No!'

Kevin's face collapsed into its usual state of crumpled martyrdom. 'THAT IS SOOO UNFAIR!'

Any second now, thought Mr Patterson, the manipulative little shit's going to try it on with his mother. Sure enough, Kevin turned and gave his mum what he obviously thought was his angelic-choirboy-butterwouldn't-melt-in-my-mouth look, which quite frankly made Mr Patterson want to smack him in the mouth. But it always seemed to have some strange primeval effect on his wife, who more often than not caved in to the boy's selfish demands. But not on this occasion she wouldn't. Oh no. If ever there was going to be a showdown between the man and the…the…half-man of the house, this was it.

'Mum…?' whined Kevin. Mrs Patterson turned to her husband, wondering – briefly – if there was some compromise that could be brokered here. It was all very well Ray laying down the law, but what it all boiled down to was that without her more sensitive approach to dealing with Kevin, her son and her husband would have long ago killed each other. Maybe she could use Kevin's interest in this Ibiza thing to motivate him into doing better at school.

'Well love, perhaps...'

She was cut short by an icy Mr Patterson. 'I said... No!' he repeated between clenched teeth, sensing at once where this was headed. Mrs Patterson looked at her husband and recognized the 'I've dug my heels in' look that she used to find so endearing. *Used* to find.

'What your father says goes,' she said, resigned.

Kevin threw his arms in the air, his martyrdom complete. 'Urg! Urg! Urg! I can't take anymore. I AM ADOPTED! My real parents couldn't possibly treat me like this. I HATE YOU!' With that, he turned heel and ran out of the house, slamming the door behind him.

Mrs Patterson folded her arms and huffed at her husband. 'I just think you leave no room to compromise,' she said, irritated and tired of the constant rows that nowadays seemed to characterize the Patterson household.

'How can you compromise with that?' protested Ray.

'Well, now he's got nothing to look forward to.'

'Which is what he deserves!' replied Ray.

Mrs Patterson felt her irritation bubble to the surface. 'Which means he'll be impossible all holiday,' she snapped. Sometimes Ray made her so mad. Why couldn't he see that the only way to deal with Kevin was to be manipulative, not belligerent? Kevin was a teenager. Being pissy was what teenagers did. It was their job. And whilst her son and her husband dug themselves into trenches and fired volleys at each other day and night it was she – the mother and the wife –

who was stuck in the middle of no-man's land, being shot at from both sides. She was tired of it. Tired of Kevin. Tired of Ray. And tired of Perry.

*Perry?*

"Scuse me, Mr and Mrs Patterson. Can I have a jam sandwich, please?'

There he was, standing in the doorway to the kitchen, looking sheepish at having witnessed the row. Perry, their son's passive alter ego, who always turned up when you least expected him.

Mrs Patterson put on a half-hearted smile and reached up to open the cupboard and get the jam down, her blouse momentarily lifting above the top of her skirt and showing a glimpse of her tummy.

Perry gulped.

Mrs Patterson was lovely.

# chapter three

Kevin hunkered down in the undergrowth, the wind howling through the trees and rain lashing the thick foliage. Water dribbled down onto his head and he pulled his collar tight around his neck to keep out the chill and the wet. It was too dark to see anything, but he heard the far-off cry of a fox. Or maybe it was an owl. Either way, it was, like him, another creature of the night.

His life was over. It might as well be. He had nothing to live for. No hope. No rescue from this eternal misery. In fact, the more he thought about it, there was no other option. He had to kill himself. That would show them. That would prove to them how much pain they'd caused. How much suffering and sadness. They'd be sorry then, wouldn't they, heh?

His mind was made up.

He would end it all here and now.

The Pattersons chose an open casket. They wanted to see as much of their beautiful boy as they could before he was taken away from them for ever. It was a brave decision, but one which they quietly thanked themselves for. The expression on the faces of the congregation said it all: Kevin *was* beautiful. Please let us look at him one more time before he's gone.

Mr Patterson, barely able to support himself under his mountain of grief, stood up and made his way to the pulpit from the front pew. The church — packed to the brim with Kevin's friends, relatives and girlfriends — mostly girlfriends, it had to be said — sniffled and sobbed as one. He wearily climbed the steps and surveyed the faces below. The terrible injustice of it all. So many gorgeous, sexually uninhibited, large-breasted women robbed of the only man who could satisfy their craven needs. His son, the hero, the genius child prodigy, so popular and so missed. Especially by the women, who on closer inspection actually made up the *entire* congregation. Women who — in honour of his son's prodigious sexual talents — had all come to the funeral in extremely skimpy clothing. In some cases, no clothing at all.

Ray cleared his throat and the sobbing subsided. He pulled from his pocket a small piece of paper. He hadn't trusted himself not to be overcome with sorrow, and so had taken the precaution of writing down his thoughts in the hearse on the way to the church.

'He was a wonderful son,' he said, his voice croaky and uneven. 'If only I had granted him his one and only wish: to go to Ibiza. If only I hadn't been so stupid and selfish...' It was all too much for him. The guilt. The loss. The envy. He broke down in tears, and the vicar rushed up to help him, guiding him back to the seat next to his wife.

Mrs Patterson looked awful. She hadn't slept a wink since Kevin's death, and she knew that she and Ray were to blame. Not just over the Ibiza issue, but everything. They'd been so hard on him, so cruel. How could anyone be expected to put up with what they did to Kevin? How they'd crushed him. How they'd snuffed out his creativity and personality as surely as if they'd pushed him under the train themselves.

The vicar solemnly took Mr Patterson's place in the pulpit. 'Kevin left us a note to remember him by,' he said. 'It is typical of the Kevin we all knew and loved, and in many cases, shagged.' There was much nodding of heads and renewed blubbering. The vicar opened the envelope he held in his hand and took out a letter. '"I am killing myself,"' he read '"because I am too good for this world. A prophet is never understood in his own land, innit. But soft, friends, don't be sad. I have gone to a far better place. A place where you never have to tidy your room. A place where your parents buy you new Nike trainers every week. I didn't mean to cause you pain, Mum, but you shouldn't have made me wash…"'

Kevin's corpse smiled even more beatifically than it already was, if that was possible, and nodded in agreement. His mother began weeping hysterically. 'Oh Kevin,' she wailed. 'Kevin, Kevin, Kevin…'

'…Kevin! Tea's ready.'

Kevin looked down at his stomach, now growling fiercely, and stood up. He stepped through the heavy undergrowth and onto the lawn, careful not to tread near the pond which Dad had covered with green netting to stop the neighbour's cat eating the goldfish. His mum was leaning out of the patio door calling to him, and through the glass he could see his dad and Perry sitting at the dinner table about to get stuck into their supper. He strolled nonchalantly up to the door, pushed past his mother and flopped down in a chair next to Perry, who was busy cramming his face with a fat jam sandwich despite the fact that he had a big plate of sausage, beans and chips in front of him.

'Alright, Kev,' said Perry with his mouth full.

'Alright, Pel,' he replied, grabbing the ketchup and squeezing it all over his dinner. His mum sat down at the table and they all ate in silence. At least it would have been silent if Perry had kept his mouth shut whilst noisily munching on his sandwich.

Kevin glanced up to see *the look* pass between his parents. The look that meant they'd been talking about him and were about to say something momentous. Fantastic, thought Kevin to himself, the Nazis have crumbled. His mum laid down her knife and fork and cleared her throat.

'Kevin. Perry. We've decided you can go to Ibiza.'

The boys grinned ecstatically, and gave each other a high five – not an easy manoeuvre when you're sitting next to one another at the dinner table. Ibiza! Here we bloody come! thought Kevin. Girls. Choons. Girls. Beaches. Girls. Girls! GIRLS!!

'Provided you get a job to pay for it.'

Kevin looked at his dad in abject horror. Provided they get a job to pay for it? What sort of sick joke was this?

'What are you talking about?' he shouted, apoplectic with instant rage. 'YOU pay for my holidays. You're my bloody parents. THAT'S WHAT YOU'RE FOR!'

'Kevin,' replied his dad, trying very hard to keep himself under control. 'Our lives are about a lot more than paying for you.'

Kevin snorted. What rubbish. 'Don't be so ridiculous,' he scoffed. What other possible purpose could there be to their pathetic, pedestrian lives other than nurturing their genius son and giving him what he needed? Which in this case was a couple of tickets to Ibiza and an apartment where he and Perry could shag girls 'til their ears bled.

Mr Patterson was about to retort when he caught a look from his wife that made him bite his tongue. Keep a lid on it Ray, he thought. Don't lose your temper. If only for the sake of your marriage. 'Pass the salt please Kevin.' he said, in as calm a voice as he could manage.

'I am not your slave!' snapped Kevin.

Mr Patterson threw his cutlery on his plate in despair. 'Look!' he said, his patience having finally run out. 'This is what happens when you try to compromise.' He said the word 'compromise' with the same disdain as you would say 'genocide', 'baby slaughter' or 'bestiality'.

'Oh, for goodness sake,' said Mrs Patterson in desperation. She'd had enough of both of them. They were as bad as each other. 'You know what the trouble with you two is? ... You're so alike!'

Kevin and his dad turned and looked at each other, mouths agape in total disgust. So alike? That was possibly the most ridiculous thing either of them had ever heard in their entire lives.

'What?' they cried in unison. 'That is SO UNFAIR!'

The following morning Kevin stormed down the street from his house with Perry dutifully in tow. The rest of the evening had ended uneventfully, with the Pattersons – and the ever-present Perry – sitting on the sofa watching television. Unfortunately, Perry had found it difficult to concentrate on *Who Wants To Be A Millionaire?* because his eyes kept getting drawn to Mrs Patterson's tits – which he had only recently noticed were very firm, very bouncy, and very, very distracting.

In an uneasy stand-off between Kevin and his dad meant that the holiday wasn't mentioned again, for fear of incurring Mrs Patterson's wrath. Perry was largely oblivious to all of this – firstly because the delicacies of family politics always passed him by, and secondly because he couldn't take his eyes off the gentle rise and fall of Mrs P's magnificent breasts.

By morning the tension had diffused a bit, and the boys decided to leave the house. 'Where are we going, Kev?' asked Perry, who'd yet to be informed of Kev's masterplan.

'To get a job. The Nazis have left us no choice.'

'Where are we gonna get a job, Kev?'

'Perry! We're cool, we're rinsin', we're large! Where do you think?' Perry didn't have a clue, but he said nothing. Kev was the man, and whatever Kev said went. In fact, Kevin had surprised even himself with the brilliance of this particular plan. He'd decided they were going in search of jobs not only befitting their cool DJ status but also likely to pay shed loads of cash for very little effort. They were going to work at High Rise Records, the mega-trendy music store in the shopping precinct. It was an obvious choice, and it stood to reason the management would be gagging to take on a couple of hip, happening dudes like themselves.

A bus journey later, they strolled through the doors of the large open-plan store and marched up to the counter, where a gaggle of shop assistants stood discussing a gig they'd all been to the night before. Kevin coughed and one of them – probably the store boss – a cool, hip thirty-something wearing the company shirt with the logo on the breast pocket, turned round.

'Yes?' he said. 'What do you want?'

'Er, well, it's like this,' said Kevin, suddenly feeling young and nervous. 'Me and Perry...'

'...that's me...'

'...wondered if you might, well, if you had a job. Two jobs. For us. To work here.'

The man stared at them open-mouthed. He didn't quite believe what he'd heard. 'You want *me* to give *you*...a job?'

Kevin nodded. 'Yes.'

'Please,' said Perry a bit squeakily.

The man suddenly burst out laughing, along with the other shop assistants. Kevin and Perry, not quite sure what the joke was about, tried to join in with some half-hearted chortles, but they both had a nagging suspicion that the joke was on them. They were right. Eventually the man wiped a tear from his eye and pointed to the door.

'Go home,' he said, 'and play with your Lego.'

If they had been dogs, they'd have had their tails between their legs and their chins on the carpet.

It couldn't get any worse.

It did.

After spending the day traipsing from store to store, it became obvious they weren't cut out for a life in retail. Or fetching shopping trolleys from car parks. Or selling the *Big Issue*. In fact, it didn't look like they were cut out for anything, except being poor and not being allowed to go on holiday to Ibiza. In desperation, they stopped at Mrs Kemp's house on the way home – an old lady down the road from Kevin's who used to babysit for him when he was little. She seemed quite pleased to see the boys, and when Kevin asked if she had any jobs she wanted doing, she pointed to her Morris Minor in the driveway and said it could do with a bit of a wash.

Neither Kevin nor Perry had ever washed a car before. In truth, there wasn't an awful lot of things they *had* washed before, themselves included. In much the same way that Kevin thought cleaning his teeth meant sucking on a bit of toothpaste, the boys figured washing a car meant apathetically throwing a soapy sponge at the bonnet for a while. After about ten minutes of aimless squirting with a couple of squeegee bottles

Kevin and Perry – dispirited and knackered – knocked on Mrs Kemp's door.

'Finished,' said Kevin when she answered, gesturing to the soapy car.

'Well done, boys,' said the old lady, who was quite clearly a bit mad if she thought the boys had done a good job. The lads put their hands out in anticipation of an enormous bag of cash for all their back-breaking hard labour. About fifty quid would be a good price, thought Kevin. But she'll probably give us a big tip as well, so it could be sixty, possibly sixty-five. The old lady reached into her handbag and put something into each of their hands. For a crazy moment Kevin thought she'd given them two hard-boiled eggs.

He looked down.

She'd given them two hard-boiled eggs.

'Thank you,' they said, on the verge of crying.

They were *never* going to get to Ibiza.


'We're not cut out for manual work, are we Kev?' said Perry despondently as they slouched along the now darkened street.

'Intellectuals aren't,' replied Kevin haughtily. 'It's just ridiculous.'

They rounded a corner and heard the all-familiar strains of 'Right Here Right Now' wafting from the window of a house. There were a few flashing lights showing through the semi-drawn curtains, and a bunch of teenagers milled around the front door, smoking and trying to look cool. One boy was collapsed against a car on the driveway, a bottle of cider in one hand, a cigar in the other and a pool of puke in his lap.

Kevin and Perry looked each other and grinned.

Like moths to a flame, they did an instant swerve, strode across the lawn and stepped over puke boy to get to the front door. And there – mesmerized by the music and sounds from within – they stepped over the threshold and entered the house.

At first glance Kevin thought there'd been some hideous mass murder. There were bodies all over the place. On the table. Under the table. On the floor. On the stairs. Everywhere he looked there were people – couples to be more precise – snogging, groping, fondling, squeezing, tweaking, stroking, undressing.

*Undressing?*

Suddenly it dawned on them that this was not the sort of party they usually went to – which always had someone's parent in the kitchen serving cider punch from a fruit bowl and a granny in the front room watching Barrymore on the telly. This was an older kids' party. This was a proper party. This was a *stiffy party*.

They stood, both with a stream of drool at their feet, transfixed by the scenes around them. Some boy had his hands down a girl's jeans and was groping her bum. A couple on the stairs were snogging so hard Kevin thought the bloke had eaten half her face. It was all a bit too much, and for fear of betraying the enormous bulges in both their trousers, they found a couple of chairs near the booze table and sat down.

'You want a drink, Kev?' croaked Perry, suddenly aware of how dry his mouth had become.

'Urrgg…' mumbled Kevin, so overcome with awe that he'd lost the power of speech.

'I said, do you want a drink?'

Kevin nodded mutely and Perry proceeded to pour them two glasses of something green and smelly from a bottle with foreign writing on it. They downed them in one, and Perry poured two more.

And that's where they stayed for the next four hours.

Staggering out of the bathroom for his first, and very long overdue, piss of the evening, Kevin stumbled down the corridor in search of somewhere to lie down. His head was pounding and the floor had an annoying habit of buckling up unexpectedly. There was also a tiny, tiny chance – just a micro-atom of a possibility – that he was going to throw up.

He reached for a door and as he was about to open it, someone tapped him on the shoulder. 'Don't go in there, mate,' said a boy. 'There's people shagging.'

*People shagging?*

Kevin gulped and his hand trembled above the handle. That meant on the other side of this piece of wood was a girl… doing it. Actually, properly *doing it*. He'd never been this close to real sex before (obviously his parents didn't do it). He felt his knees tremble.

Kevin smirked at the boy in a way which he hoped looked grown-up, and pointed at another door. 'How about that one?' he asked nonchalantly. He really, really needed to lie down now.

'That's just sad acts sleeping.'

Kevin scoffed knowingly, but as soon as the boy turned away Kevin gratefully opened the door and lurched in.

Carnage, just like the rest of the house. Bodies littered the floor like a scene from some Crimean battlefield. Kevin looked longingly at the bed in the corner which was occupied by a boy snoring loudly. The boy made a startled snorting noise, rolled over in his sleep and promptly fell comatose onto the carpet. Kevin took his chance and – treading as carefully as he could given his sense of balance was all a bit screwy – fell onto the bed. This was just what he needed. Horizontal.

He was just beginning to doze off when the door to the room burst open and he heard a girl's voice on the landing. 'Aw man, my head. I've gotta crash, man.'

'Later Sharon – great party!' came a reply.

'Cheers,' said Sharon, who then staggered into view in the doorway, surveying the slaughter with a low moan. Kevin, who was watching this through half-closed eyes, thought it might be a good idea to pretend to be asleep. The girl picked her way across the floor, aiming for the bed, and Kevin's pulse started racing.

Bloody hell, he thought to himself in disbelief. She's gonna get into bed with me. Bed! That's where people have sex. Bloody bloody hell.

The girl made it to the other side of the room and slumped on the edge of the mattress. Obviously very pissed, she began slowly pulling her clothes off until – more by luck than anything else – she was down to her bra and knickers.

OH MY GOD OH MY GOD OH MY GOD, thought Kevin, the blood pounding in his ears and a very strange tingling sensation running down his legs. Oh my God. She's going to get in, she's going to get in.

Sharon lifted up the covers and saw Kevin curled up and sleeping on the side nearest the wall. She grunted in disgust, and Kevin, seeing this as an ideal opportunity to introduce himself, opened one eye and went 'Awright?' Too pissed to even bother throwing him out, the girl collapsed next to Kevin, who froze like a rabbit in headlights.

The duvet sprang upwards above his crotch.

For the rest of the night the girl tossed and turned and fidgeted and kicked and twisted and grunted and snored and farted.

Kevin didn't move a muscle. All night he kept formulating plan after plan of how he could get off with this girl – this *semi-naked girl lying next to him in bed* – but for the life of him he couldn't conceive of any possible way to get things started. His stiffy remained defiantly upright and on a couple of occasions the girl banged it with her elbow, making Kevin's eyes water and his bladder hurt.

But still he didn't move. All he could do was stare at her bum, at her tits, at her belly, at her thighs, at everything, in mute wonder.

By now dawn had come and a grey light was seeping into the room through the curtains. Kevin was just wondering what to do if the girl woke up when the door opened and Perry's face appeared. Kevin had completely forgotten about Perry. After five hours of intense sensory overload it was all he could do to remember his own name. When Perry saw Kevin, his eyes popped in disbelief.

Kevin was in bed. With a girl. With no clothes on. And Kevin was grinning. And...and...and...wow.

'Kev...!' he said reverently.

'Oh, morning Perry,' replied Kevin, trying to sound as if being found in bed with a semi-naked girl was the most natural thing in the world for him. He turned to Sharon – still snoring – and then gave Perry a knowing wave.

Nuff said.


The boys crept out of the house as quietly as they could, stepping over the victims of the party and weaving a way to the front door.

'Did you shag her?' asked Perry, still not quite believing what he just saw.

'Yeah, course,' said Kevin, who felt a bit guilty lying to his best mate but knowing full well this was an ideal opportunity to *really* improve his reputation – especially at school.

'You shagged Sharon?' asked Perry again. He'd recognized the girl from the bus to school and simply

31

couldn't get his head around the fact that Kevin wasn't a virgin anymore.

'Only three times,' said Kevin, trying to sound modest.

They made it to the front door and opened it to a cold, misty morning, oblivious to the fact that lying at the foot of the stairs, pretending to be asleep, was Stacey, Sharon's best friend.

And she'd heard every word.

# chapter four

Perry was worried. Kevin had shagged someone, and he hadn't. He didn't know why it unsettled him so much, but it did. Maybe it was the thought that Kevin might not want to be his mate anymore — him still being a virgin and all that.

Perry didn't know what he'd do without Kev as his mate. They'd been friends for ever, but since Perry's mum and dad got divorced he seemed to almost live at the Pattersons. He liked them, Mr and Mrs Patterson. They made him feel welcome and they were nice.

Mrs Patterson especially.

Perry decided to stop thinking about Mrs P in case something happened in his trousers. He turned to Kevin, who oddly didn't seem very cheerful for having got his first shag last night. 'So you've done it with a girl then Kev?' asked Perry. If he couldn't get a shag himself he was determined to hear all about it from someone who had.

'Yeah, I stuck it up her good!' said Kevin, thrusting his hips forward and then nearly tripping over.

Perry nodded. He knew now why he felt so depressed. Kevin had got a shag and so he wouldn't want to go on holiday. It stood to reason. 'Does that mean you don't want to go to Ibiza now?' he asked.

'Eh?' said Kevin.

'Now that you've done it with a girl, you don't need to go to Ibiza for a guaranteed shag,' noted Perry. 'S'alright, mate, I'll get a shag here, probably.' Perry knew this was patently untrue, but he didn't want his mate to feel bad about bailing out of Ibiza.

'No, no, we'll still go to Ibiza,' said Kevin. 'I can always do *more* shagging.'

Perry hadn't thought of that. Of course. Kevin could always do some *more* shagging. He suddenly felt very relieved. 'Oh thanks, Kevin. You're a mate!' He punched Kevin on the arm as a mark of male respect, only he did it a bit too hard and Kevin winced in pain. Then Perry remembered how they'd ended up at the party in the first place.

'But we still gotta get the money, Kev. How we gonna get the money?'

Kevin stopped dead in his tracks, and still rubbing his arm, turned to Perry with his best 'I got shagged last night and so I'm a genius' look on his face. 'We can earn our money on the streets where the *real* people are! Let's do a gig!'

'Sounds a bit tinny, Kev.'

'Doesn't matter,' said Kevin, cranking up the volume switch on his beat-box until the walls of the shopping precinct thumped with their kickin' choons. Well, the walls would have thumped, if Kevin's stereo had been a bit bigger than a small packet of biscuits. Or if the stereo had been running on four trillion megawatts instead of two batteries he'd nicked out of the TV remote control. The quiet retail calm of the shopping mall was not so much shattered as mildly scratched by something that sounded like a toy lorry reversing over a packet of crisps.

'Cool!' grinned Perry. It was the first gig he'd ever been to, even if it was his own.

'You ready?' shouted Kevin.

'Let's do it!' said Perry, all fired up. They grabbed their mikes and launched into the opening lines of the Vocal Live Remix (Mega Mix Monsta) of 'Big Girl'.

Already struggling to cope with the output from the tape, the overloaded speakers distorted under the extra strain of Kev and Pel's frantic shouting. Two shoppers unfortunate enough to be standing nearby gave them a withering look and walked off shaking their heads. Kev didn't care. This was just like the New Radicals' video. Once all the boring farts went away, they were going to be swamped by loads of really cool people who'd dance around them and thrust fifty pound notes in his trousers. The manager of Top Man would probably come out and give them some jackets just for being so fantastic. And then they'd have to run through the mall being pursued by girls with tight pants and big tits. It was going to be very satisfactory.

As it was, all they had right now was two old ladies sitting on a bench eating strawberry bonbons.

'What are they doing?' asked the one with the blue hair.

'I think they're selling something,' replied her friend, who had a hairy lip and – even by old lady standards – smelled rather peculiar.

'Can we get any of it for free?'

'I don't know dear. I'll ask.' She pulled herself upright and shuffled over to Kevin, who tried to ignore her – difficult because she had quite an unpleasant whiff about her. 'Hello, young man,' she said. 'What are you selling?'

'What?' shouted Kevin.

'I said, what are you selling?'

Kevin shook his head. What was he selling? His life, that's what he was selling. Prostituting his beautiful talent because his bloody parents were bloody bastards who hated him, which was OK because he hated them too and when he was rich enough he was going to have them bloody well locked up in a private bloody prison.

He bent down and turned off the stereo. 'We,' said Kevin, with great patience and self control 'are DJ mix-masters. I'm DJ Kev and this is DJ Pel. This is a gig, for ravers. We are not selling anything except our talent, which is quite expensive actually.'

'Two quid,' grinned Perry, sticking his hand under the old lady's chin.

'Is it Guy Fawke's Night then?' asked the old lady. 'Are you the Guy?'

'No, I'm not the Guy,' snorted Kevin.

'His name's Kevin,' said Perry, trying to help.

'I'm sorry, dear. I don't have two pounds. You can have a bonbon if you like.'

Kevin and Perry looked at each other. 'Thank you very much,' they mumbled into their chests as the old lady popped a sweet into each of their hands and then went and sat down next to her friend. Kevin and Perry chewed their sweets for a bit, and then went through the extravagant motions of rewinding the tape and starting over again.

By now a smattering of people had stopped to listen, some of them boys Perry recognized from the bus he and Kevin caught to go to school. Those who did stop kept their distance, and pretended they weren't paying any attention. They didn't want anyone to think they were listening to these two desperately sad kids. That would be too embarrassing.

Sharon stood at the till with Stacey and paid for her lipstick. She was still spitting mad. That stupid little twat had been going round telling everyone she'd slept with him. With him! She'd rather shag a diseased donkey than that immature spotty little git. Alright, so she was wellied the night of the party, but not so out of it she would completely forget she was a member of the human race. What a moron...

'What are you gonna do if you see him?' asked Stacey, grateful to be involved in such an outstandingly brilliant drama. There hadn't been goss this good since Linda Chisholm thought she was pregnant after shagging that greasy Greek bloke at the kebab shop. Telling everyone about that one (in the strictest confidence, of course) had been the highlight of her half-term. As it turned out, Linda wasn't pregnant, but it didn't matter anyway. Stacey had got plenty of mileage out of the rumour, and when you're the source of good goss, your cool-rating goes right through the ceiling.

'I'm gonna smash his ugly little face in,' replied Sharon. The woman behind the till made an audible tutt, and Sharon retaliated with her best Jerry-Springer-talk-to-my-hand-cos-my-face-ain't-listening look. Since the woman had never seen Jerry Springer, she just thought Sharon had a bit of a crick in her neck. Or maybe the girl needed glasses. Difficult to tell when they're that age, she thought to herself, they're all freaks.

Sharon stashed the new lippy in her bag, and the girls walked out of Boots into the shopping mall. From somewhere further down the cavernous hallway came the sound of a stereo, and a great deal of shouting. Curious, the girls followed the noise until they turned a corner and surveyed the scene before them.

Stacey grinned. Oh boy. This was almost too good to be true.

Standing in the middle of the hall were the two boys from the party, bouncing up and down and yelling into a home-made karaoke machine with all the musical talent of her pet dog.

'That's them,' said Stacey.

'You what?' asked Sharon.

'That's them. That ginger one. He's the one who said he shagged you.'

Before Stacey could say anything more, Sharon stomped away across the hall, her heels clacking frantically on the marble floor like manic maracas. Stacey tried to keep up, but Sharon was on a mission. And when Sharon was on a mission, she was unstoppable.

Kevin didn't know what hit him. One minute he was bangin' out some monsta choons (to what was now, without doubt, an almost-possibly-reasonable-sized crowd), the next he was face-to-face with a screaming lunatic in a tight blouse. It took about a microsecond to recognize her. After all, he'd spent all night staring at her tits. It was the girl from the party.

Oh God. The girl from the party. Oh God oh God oh God oh God. Bloody hellfire and pants.

Stacey, who'd caught up by now, went straight to the stereo and pulled out the plug. The precinct descended into ominous silence.

'I want a word with you,' spat Sharon, hands clenched into fists, just itching to slug him one.

Kevin cringed. 'Oh hello darlin', how's it going?' he mumbled, still trying desperately to maintain the illusion of a couple who had only recently bonked the entire night away.

'Did you say you shagged me last night?' shouted Sharon. Kevin felt his face flush. But this was no ordinary blush. It was some kind of freak-of-nature uber-blush. It felt like every drop of blood in his body had been pumped under high pressure into his face, which was now a bright, sweaty crimson and in danger of rupturing any second.

'No,' he mumbled, paralysed with shame and worried his head was about to explode.

'Yeah, you bloody did! Stacey heard you!' Stacey – who'd squared up behind Sharon for extra effect – gave Kevin the sort of stare usually reserved for lumps of dogshit on the soles of your shoes.

'No I didn't,' Kevin squeaked, glancing over at Perry who was looking very confused indeed.

'I wouldn't shag you in a million years, you sad twat,' said Sharon. 'You say anything like that again and I'll smack you!' She took one last sneering look at Kevin and spat, 'You virgin!' With that, she spun on her heels and marched off with Stacey clattering behind her.

Kevin felt a million eyes bearing down on him. The precinct had come to a complete halt at Sharon's outburst and now an uneasy hush filled the hall. Someone giggled.

'You said you shagged her three times,' said Perry, not quite sure what to make of it all.

'Shut up, Perry,' snapped Kevin, his face still burning. 'I'm getting out of here. This place is full of losers!'

He picked up the stereo and the mikes, and with his head tucked into his chest, strutted away from the gawping shoppers, leaving Perry to hurriedly pick up the few coins that they themselves had put into a shoe box on the ground.

Kevin sped up.

He didn't want to be seen crying. Not by Perry.

# chapter five

Perry found Kevin sitting on a bench outside, clutching his stereo on his lap. He went over and flopped down next to him, and they sat for a while saying nothing. Perry didn't care what those girls had just said. It didn't matter to him whether Kevin had shagged Sharon or not. He knew what he'd seen with his own eyes – Kev, in a bed, with a girl who didn't have any clothes on. That was so much further than Perry had ever gone with a girl, it was worthy of enormous respek. And maybe Kev had genuinely thought he'd shagged her. Perry – whose life skirted perilously along the edge between fantasy and reality anyway – knew that sometimes if you thought about things hard enough they kind of became real, at least in your head. And if things aren't real there, where are they real?

'Yeah, cos the girls don't appreciate our musical genius here, do they Kev?' said Perry, in an attempt to make Kev feel better.

'Naah,' said Kevin, suddenly feeling very sorry himself again. All he could think about was the humiliation of having that girl call him a virgin in front of everyone. Being told he was a sad twat by a girl he sort of fancied. And it wasn't as if he really deserved it. It was just a little lie, a tiny weeny exaggeration for Perry and no one else. He hadn't gone round telling people he'd shagged Sharon. It was just something he'd said for fun. He hadn't meant it to be taken seriously.

Things were getting truly desperate.

By the time they got back to Kevin's house, they were both thoroughly depressed. There didn't seem to be any way out, nothing that would offer them a chance to go to Ibiza. For both of them, the holiday had taken on a symbolic importance. It didn't matter that their school reports were crap, that they had spots and that girls didn't like them. If they could just get to Ibiza everything would be alright. Then things would be…cleaner, brighter, better. Both knew their lives would forever be different if they could only get there. His parents just didn't understand it. How could they?

'What are we gonna do, Kev?' asked Perry as they turned the corner into Kevin's road.

'I don't know, Perry. It's all gone Pete Tong!' said Kevin.

Perry, suddenly robbed of Kevin's contagious self-confidence, saw the whole awful mess for what it was. A life without girlfriends. A life without sex. A life without hope. His bottom lip began to tremble and for the first time in as long as he could remember, he wanted his mum.

'Excuse me,' said a voice from behind them. They turned around to see Kevin's postman standing holding an envelope. 'Registered letter for your father. Can you sign for it?'

'Sure,' said Kevin, without thinking. He grabbed the postman's clipboard and, under the small box marked Patterson, signed his name, a hugely intricate baroque nest of swirls, whirls, twisty bits, underlinings, dots and illegible lumps that filled the entire page. Kevin liked his signature. It was very unique.

He handed the board back to the postie who —
scowling and wondering why this boy had just scribbled
out all the other signatures on the page — handed over
a white envelope and walked off.

Kevin and Perry looked at the letter.

YOUR BRAND NEW CREDIT CARD, it shouted in
enormous letters across the top.

Kevin's face lit up. 'Perry! We're saved!'

Perry didn't quite see how. But if Kev said they were
saved, they were saved.

They turned tail and headed back into town. Perry
didn't dare ask Kevin what the plan was. It would only
make him look a bit thick for not getting it. He was
happy just to go with the flow, and Kevin was definitely
flowing now. The usual bounce was back in his step, and
when Kevin was happy, Perry was happy.

They stood outside the entrance to the bank in the
High Street and Kevin opened the envelope. 'We get the
money and go to Ibiza. Today. Sorted.' He pulled a
Gold MasterCard from inside the letter. Perry gulped.

'But that's your dad's credit card isn't it, Kev!' he
gasped, the details of Kevin's plan now becoming dread-
fully apparent. 'It's stealing! We'll be sent to prison and
get buggered by bigger boys!' This had preyed on
Perry's mind since the incident in the newsagent's. He
was desperate to lose his virginity, but not to some
remand prisoner called Slasher at Feltham Young
Offenders Institute. He'd watched *Scum* on video. He
knew what went on.

Kevin shrugged dismissively. 'You will. You're small.
I'll be alright.'

Perry looked bleakly at the card and wondered
what he was getting himself into. He'd trust Kev over
anything, but this just seemed a bit...mental.

Too late to do anything about it now, though. Kevin had already strode into the bank and joined the queue for the counter. Since it looked like Kevin was going ahead with it anyway, Perry thought the least he could do was go on the holiday with him.

He took a deep breath, crossed his fingers and went in.

'We'll pay him back when we're famous DJs,' said Kevin when Perry got to his side, in a vain attempt to make him feel a bit better. 'You in or out?'

'I'm in,' replied Perry reluctantly. If being buggered by Slasher was the price he had to pay for getting a shag with a girl in Ibiza, so be it. They stepped up to the counter, Perry's hands subconsciously covering his bum in anticipation of the awful rogering he was bound to get in the showers of D-Block.

Kevin looked at the woman behind the counter and felt a familiar rustling in his underpants. She was completely shag-a-delic. His eyes kept getting drawn to her fantastically pert boobies and Kevin fought to keep his erection under control. This was important. He could get all the stiffies he wanted once he was in Ibiza. Until then, he needed to focus on getting the cash and legging it out of the country – undoubtedly pursued by top sleuths at Scotland Yard who'd be told to drop all their investigations into Sir Jeremy Parlo, the infamous international jewel thief, and hunt down Kevin the DJ instead.

He gave the woman his best 'I've just been sent my new Gold MasterCard' smile, expecting a nice smile back and the offer of large bags of cash.

She screamed.

For a moment Kevin thought he'd been busted. Maybe the postman had reported the card stolen and his photograph had been sent round all the local banks. Or maybe she could see the beginnings of his stiffy. Or maybe there was a bloke standing next him wearing a donkey jacket and pointing a shotgun at her head.

*Oh fuck...*

'Shut your noise or I'll blow your face off!' said the shotgun bloke to the woman behind the counter.

She shut it.

Then the bloke swung the gun round and pointed it at Kevin and Perry. 'You two! Move! NOW!' He gestured to one of the financial advisor's desks. The boys – who couldn't quite believe they'd had the good fortune to be caught up in a real bank robbery – nodded and shuffled backwards. The robber waved his gun at the rest of the customers in the bank. 'Right, put your hands up and keep your mouth shut!' Spotting Kevin and Perry, who had shuffled back as far as they could but were now frozen to the spot, as he swung back round, he said, 'You stupid? Sit down and put your hands up!'

They nodded fervently and slid into a couple of swivel chairs behind the desk, hands still firmly in the air. The reality of having the twin barrels of a shotgun pointed at their heads began to sink in and Perry gave a little whimper.

The robber turned back to the girl behind the counter and threw her a sack. 'You fill it up!' She leant forward to reach the cash box under her desk, and started stuffing the sack as quickly as she could with money. As she did so, Kevin and Perry got a spectacular view of her cleavage, magnificently framed by the saucy black lace of her bra.

Kevin's stiffy, lurking in standby mode, suddenly sprang energetically into life, whacking the underside of the desk. At least it would have whacked the underside of the desk if the big red 'Robber Alert Panic Button' hadn't got in the way.

The room exploded into a cacophony of flashing lights and lunatic alarm bells. Kevin – hands still in the air – looked down into his lap in despair. This was, without any doubt at all, the most embarrassing stiffy he'd ever had in his life. The robber – who was about to grab the sack full of cash from the girl, spun around in a panic. How on earth had the alarm been set off? Everyone had their hands in the air. No one could possibly have triggered the button.

This wasn't in the plan. Running out the front door with more money than Bill Gates – now *that* was his plan. Getting banged up for armed robbery was definitely not top of his list of things to do when he was eating his breakfast this morning.

He stood frozen in indecision. Leg it? Grab the money, then leg it? Shoot someone? Shoot someone and then leg it? It was a delay that cost him dear. Everywhere he looked steel shutters were coming down over the tills and the door. Furious, he scanned the customers to see who would make a good hostage. As his eyes met the spotty kid sitting at the desk, he noticed a mysterious red light flashing underneath the desktop.

*The little twat had set the alarm off!*

But how? The kid's hands were still in the air. He walked up to the desk, and keeping his gun aimed at the little shit's head, knelt down to look at the alarm.

What he saw next earned him the nickname 'Boner Briggs' for the next three-and-a-half years he spent in Wormwood Scrubs at Her Majesty's Pleasure. The kid had an erection – a big old hard-on by the looks of it – that had bashed the alarm button. He looked at the kid in downright disbelief, who grimaced apologetically.

Boner Briggs – a superstitious man at the best of times – flopped to the floor, threw his gun away and put his head in his hands. Beaten by a stiffy.

If ever there was a reason to give up armed robbery, this was it.

By the time the police had sprung the release mechanism on the door shutters, Boner was sitting in the corner blubbing quietly to himself, a junior loans officer (grade III trainee) standing over him with the shotgun in his hands.

Kevin had been lauded by the customers and staff alike for managing to set the alarm off, although no one except him and Boner knew how he'd done it. That was fine by Kevin, who had no intention of detailing the activity in his underpants, least of all for the girl in the lacy bra.

He was getting his millionth pat on the back when the bank manager appeared at his side clutching a wad of bank notes, neatly bound in a thin strip of purple paper that had '£1000' printed on it.

'On behalf of the bank,' he said portentously, 'Thank you very much. Enjoy that reward money.'

Kevin looked at Perry. Perry looked at the reward money. Kevin looked at the reward money. Perry looked at Kevin. They both looked at the bank manager.

'And if ever you want a job,' continued the grey man in the grey suit, 'you give me a ring. Banking offers many exciting career opportunities for virgins such as yourselves.'

'Thank you...yes...thank you, please...thanks!' they stammered together, only to stop in bewilderment and shame as what he had actually just said slowly dawned on them.

'Thank you very much,' said Mr Patterson, waving to the reporter and photographer from the local paper who were retreating down the drive towards their car. 'We'll look out for it next week!'

He closed the door and came back into the lounge, where Kevin and Perry stood, chests puffed up and chins held high. TEENAGE HEROES THWART HIGH STREET ROBBERY was the headline destined for next week's paper. Mr Patterson couldn't quite believe it.

'We're very proud of you both,' said Kevin's mum, pouring out some tea in the kitchen. 'It was really public spirited.'

'"Kevin" and "public-spirited". I never thought I'd hear those words together,' said Mr Patterson, a remark which earned him a scowl from Kevin and an icy glare from his wife.

Kevin's mum reached into a drawer in the dresser and fished out an envelope. 'We've got a present for you.' She smiled and patted the envelope on the table. VIRGIN AIRLINES, it said, in big red and white letters.

'How did you know we're still virgins?' blurted Perry.

'What?' asked Mr Patterson.

'Oh...nothing,' mumbled Perry, realizing what he'd said.

'Well?' said Mrs Patterson. 'Aren't you going to thank Dad?'

'What?' said Kevin.

'Well he's paid for our tickets, so you can spend your reward money on holiday.'

Kevin looked at his mother in horror. 'What do you mean...*our* tickets?'

'We're coming too,' replied his mother. Kevin and Perry's faces simultaneously fell twenty feet.

'You didn't think we'd let you go on your own did you?' quipped his dad scornfully.

Kevin was stunned. What was going on? When he couldn't afford to go, they refused to buy his ticket for him. Now he could afford to go, and they were going to ruin it by coming with him. The bastards!

'That...' he shouted, working up to a really big finish, 'is SO *UNFAIR!*'

Perry sat on Kevin's bed scratching his head and wondering what to say. He didn't mind Mr and Mrs Patterson coming on holiday with them. In fact, he didn't mind at all. Mrs Patterson especially. He searched for the right words that would make Kev feel better. 'Never mind, Kev' he said, giving up.

'Bastards...' huffed Kevin.

'We don't have to hang out with them,' said Perry, finally articulating why he thought the holiday would still be alright. 'If they've paid for the flights it leaves us more dosh for top gear!' He chuckled, waving the reward money at Kevin. Though he thought so himself, that was a truly cool idea. Nikes, jackets, portable CD players, digital camcorders, hats, dockers, Prodigy Dirtchamber remixes. He was holding one hell of a lot of gear in his hand, even if he hadn't gone out and got it yet.

Kevin sat up. 'Perry. You're right,' he said, finding it mentally taxing to agree with his parents even when it worked to his advantage. 'Let us prepare!'

They got up and left the house, off to spend more money than they'd ever done in their entire lives.

Next stop, Ibiza.

# chapter six

Kevin and Perry stood outside the arrivals lounge watching the surge of holidaymakers spill into the baking heat of the Ibizan summer. This was so much better than they'd ever thought it could be. Wherever they looked it was girls, girls, girls. Girls in T-shirts. Girls in bikinis. Girls in tiny, tiny shorts. They had stiffies that had started at Gatwick and showed no signs of abating four hours later. But the boys didn't care. Togged up in their best kit – Calvin Kleins, Stussy T-shirts, Reebok sweatshirts, thick puffa jackets and hats – they were sweaty, ridiculous, but happy.

Perry couldn't have been happier if he'd died and gone to heaven. Maybe he had. Perhaps he'd been shot during the bank robbery and this was all some weird afterlife where angels had thongs and pierced bellybuttons instead of wings and a harp. If he didn't get to a bathroom soon, something unexpected was going to go off in his Calvins. But just when his sensory overload couldn't get more extreme, the crowd near the coachstop parted and for a moment he got a glimpse of two girls that made his heart stop.

'Kev,' he whispered. 'Look. The girls of our dreams.' He pointed at two girls who were walking towards them pushing a luggage cart and chewing gum.

They were beautiful. No, not just beautiful. Goddesses of love.

OK, so they were a bit spotty. And one was quite chubby. And the other had this sort of depressed, miserable look about her. And yeah, fair enough, they looked gawky and unsure of themselves and lost in the sea of super-cool, professional ravers milling around the car park. But...but...there was an undeniable magic about them that had both Kevin and Perry rooted to the spot.

'Boys! Over here, now!' Mr Patterson's voice boomed across the car park and a few heads turned to see who was shouting. Kevin winced in embarrassment. His parents. Oh God, what a twisted torture. He took off his hat and threw it to the ground.

'This is the worst holiday of my life!' he groaned. His dad shouted at them again, and Kevin begrudgingly picked up his hat and trudged off in the direction of the taxi his parents had hailed, head lowered and spirits lower. This whole thing was going to be a nightmare. He should never have agreed to come. He turned to get some moral support from Perry following two steps behind, but his fellow DJ was still straining to see the girls who had disappeared behind a coach.

But it wasn't the girls that had Perry straining to look over Kevin's shoulder. While he'd been scanning the faces to try and see their love angels, an enormous white stretch limousine had pulled up in front of the airport exit and a big bloke had jumped out of the driver's seat and run round to open the door. And who had walked up to the car pushing a cart full of record cases with a couple of lovely looking ladies on each arm? Only a face that had been scorched onto Perry's brain from a thousand editions of *Mixmag*, *Ministry of Sound* magazine and *Smash Hits*.

DJ Eye Ball Paul, the greatest living club DJ on the entire planet. And he was standing right next to them. He looked even better than he did on TV – taller, ganglier, more goateed, blonder and more sort of… scuzzier. Perry grabbed Kevin's arm and pointed at the limo. 'Kev! Look!'

Kevin took off his sunglasses and squinted at the car. 'It's superstar DJ Eye Ball Paul!' They watched in stunned amazement as the DJ nodded at his driver.

'Tits up Big Baz, 'avin it large!' said the legend.

The boys took a tentative step forward and gave the DJ a nervous thumbs up. 'Alright, Eye Ball Paul?' said Kevin, painfully aware that he was in the presence of greatness. Eye Ball Paul turned and looked at the boys with a look of enormous disdain, deciding for a moment whether or not he should deign to talk to them. He leant forward as if to whisper something of great importance, and promptly belched loudly in their faces.

'Cool!' said Perry, impressed that someone as massive as DJ Eye Ball Paul still enjoyed burping.

'Hur! Brilliant!' sniggered Kevin. The DJ turned to his two female escorts – both of whom looked like Southend Scrubbers – and ordered them into the car.

'Muff. Wankette. You dirty little club babes. Get in.' The girls slipped wordlessly into the back of the limo, giving Perry a great view of their knickers as they slid into their seats. He grunted involuntarily and grabbed his crotch.

'You doin' some sets out here then?' asked Kevin, trying very hard to sound like a fellow DJ discussing the subtleties of the Ibiza club scene – of which he knew absolutely nothing.

'Bangin' sets, little boys. Top choons, cool mixes. That's Eye Ball Paul.' The DJ kept glancing over the boys' shoulders, utterly disinterested in anything these little pricks might have to say to him but keen to make sure that idiot Big Baz didn't smash up his records getting them into the boot of the car. 'Oi! Big Baz!' he barked. 'Careful, you clumsy twat. Them choons ain't spaggage!' Kevin laughed knowledgeably – he'd lost count of the number of times *his* roadies had spanked up his record collection...

'Yeah, we'll probably be doing some sets and all, probably, cos we're DJs too...' he said optimistically.

'Yeah?' replied Eye Ball Paul as he got into the car, wondering to himself whether he had time to shag both these little tarts in the back of the limo before he got to his apartment.

'Kevin! Perry!' came an all too familiar voice from behind them. The boys turned around to see Kev's mum waiting by the taxi and waving frantically at them. 'Hurry up, boys!' she yelled.

Eye Ball Paul leaned out the car and sniggered. 'Mummy's calling little boys,' he goaded. 'Hurry up. She is one lippy bitch!' He cackled with laughter, slammed the door, and the limo screeched away in a cloud of dust and fag butts.

'Later Eye Ball Paul,' said Kevin. He turned to Perry. 'He's such a nice bloke.'

'He's our new best mate, isn't he Kev?'

'Yeah, he really likes us and if we can get him to hear our mixes maybe he'll let us do a set with him...'

'... and shag his birds...'

'... and shag all the birds we want!' said Kevin confidently. Perry grunted in agreement and Kevin grinned. 'This is the best holiday of my life,' he crowed as they strutted towards the waiting taxi and his parents.

A short taxi ride later and they pulled up outside a pretty-looking apartment by the seafront. It was sited above a little restaurant, and had twin balconies – one for each of the bedrooms – dripping in flowers which hung over the edges in great splashes of red and yellow. Kevin's dad paid for the cab and they carried their suitcases up the staircase by the side of the building and into the apartment.

'Oh Ray,' said Kevin's mum as they went in. 'This is lovely.' As Kev's parents looked appreciatively around their accommodation, Kevin and Perry stomped straight into the bedroom with the twin beds, dumped their bags, turned tail and immediately strutted back out again towards the door.

'See you on the beach,' said Mr Patterson cheerfully.

'I don't think so,' jeered Kevin.

'We're right by the sea,' said Mrs Patterson, pointing out the big bay windows. 'You've got to go to the beach.'

'Yeah, but not *your* beach. We are going to *the* beach.' Kevin reached into his jacket and pulled out a crumpled copy of *Mixmag* – the issue with 'Ibiza Special' on the front cover in silvery writing. 'The beach that you don't even know about because you're *nearly dead!*'

Mr Patterson – who'd tried very hard to keep his temper on a short leash since they'd left early that morning – suddenly lost it. He'd just about had enough of Kevin's truculence, a constant high-level whining and arguing that was more than anyone was expected to take – especially a parent. 'How dare you speak to your mother like that!' he snarled. But it was too late. Kevin and Perry had already scuttled down the steps and jumped into a cab – the same one that hadn't even had time to pull away since dropping them off. 'KEVIN!' bellowed his father over the balcony. '*KEVIN!! I'm talking to you!*'

Furious, he stepped back into the apartment, thankful he wasn't a violent man. If he was, Kevin would be in

53

traction and he'd be in prison by now. 'That boy's going to ruin our holiday,' he stormed, throwing a suitcase on the bed and unzipping it frenetically.

'No, Ray,' replied Mrs Patterson, whose temper had also reached breaking point. '*You* are going to ruin *my* holiday!'

'What?' he responded, suddenly feeling the sands of righteousness shift beneath his feet.

'He's a teenager,' snarled Mrs Patterson, so angry she couldn't even look him in the face as she busied herself unpacking her case. 'He's like every other teenager. Somewhere, Ray, there's a universe with a planet identical to our own, but all their children are nightmares. At thirteen they swap their kids for ours. At eighteen they give ours back. For those five years we have an alien living with us and there's nothing we can do!'

'But he's driving me mad,' offered Ray, wanting to defend himself but knowing full well once his wife went into one it was best just to stand back and let her fizzle herself out, like a dangerous firework.

'Only if you let him, Ray. This is my holiday too! I've got the sun, the sea, a beautiful place to stay and I want to enjoy it with my kind, loving husband. Not some raving lunatic!' With that, she burst into tears, threw the now-empty case under the bed and walked onto the balcony. Ray sighed and sat on the bed.

She was right. Of course she right. She always was. This was their holiday as much as it was Kevin and Perry's. And who was supposed to be the grown-up here? Who had the greater responsibility to keep things under control? By letting Kevin get to him, Kevin had won.

He looked at his wife leaning on the balustrade, staring out to sea, and thought how beautiful she looked with the sun in her hair, and how much he loved her. It wasn't right for her to be the innocent casualty of all of this aggravation between him and Kevin. It wasn't fair. She deserved better.

He reached into the duty-free bag and pulled out a bottle. A nice glass of wine, that'll help. And maybe a romantic walk along the seafront. He smiled to himself and went to fetch two glasses from the kitchen cupboard. Yes, a nice romantic walk. That would be great.

He took the wine onto the balcony, put the glasses on a small table and put his arms around her waist. 'I'm sorry,' he said. 'You're right. It is a beautiful place.' She turned and they smiled at each other.

'It's alright, Ray. I just want us to have a special time.'

'We will,' he promised. 'We will.'

They kissed — a pretty saucy kiss as it happened — and Mr Patterson put his hands on his wife's lovely, curvy bottom.

Maybe the walk could wait 'til later.


The boys had jumped into the cab and waved the magazine under the driver's nose, the noise of Mr Patterson's frantic screaming immediately muffled the moment they slammed the door shut.

'The beach please please thank you,' said Kevin. The driver nodded — his English patchy but his understanding of spoddy kids out on the pull more than adequate — and drove off.

They were there within ten minutes. The cab dropped them at the top of a cliff, where a scraggy footpath led down the steep hillside to the bay below. The boys leapt out to survey the scene.

It was magic. The beach was heaving with young people sunbathing, drinking, and dancing to the various strains of music drifting up from below. There were pedalloes, water-skiers, windsurfers, and — more important than all of these put together – girls. Hundreds of them.

They walked down the path to the beach, which for a while took them out of sight of the throng as it hugged the cliff. But then, emerging from between two large rocks, the boys found themselves standing in the middle of the beach, surrounded by what they'd seen from the cliff-top.

Breasts. More breasts than either of them had ever seen, in real life, in print or on video. Naked breasts. Big breasts. Little breasts. Pointy breasts. Reliably on cue, their stiffies boinged into action and the boys stood gaping at the beach with embarrassingly obvious tent poles in their trousers.

Standing on an Ibizan beach in mid-August wearing thick padded puffa jackets and the kind of clothing layers you normally only associate with trans-Siberian explorers did not make the boys feel even the slightest bit self-conscious. But two irrepressible boners did. They glanced uneasily at each other's trousers and, without saying a word, knelt on the sand and began frantically digging two stiffy holes. Once dug, they fell forward, impaled themselves into the beach, and relaxed.

'Oi, Kevin, look!' said Perry. He pointed across the beach. 'It's the girls from the airport!' Sure enough, walking along the sea's edge were their two Venusian beauties – topless! The boys gawped in silent joy as the girls walked right past them. Their stiffies, which were full to bursting point, got improbably stiffier.

'Let's go and stand quite near them, so they can get interested in us,' suggested Kevin, whose grasp of chatting-up girls was patchy at best, and non-existent the rest of the time.

'Good idea,' said Perry, who tried to stand up, but to his immediate dismay discovered he was well and truly snagged in his stiffy hole. 'I'm hooked in, Kevin,' he hissed between clenched teeth. Kevin tried to lift himself up and realized he was in the same predicament.

'Me, too,' he whispered, feeling slightly panicky. What if the tide came in? They'd drown, a bizarre death by hard-on, virgins killed by their own erections. 'We'll have to get to the sea to cool off.' With enormous effort they grabbed the sand in front of them and dragged themselves forward towards the sea, a painfully slow — and painful — advance that left two deeply ploughed furrows behind them like the wake from a couple of beach-bound ocean liners.

Once at the sea, they floated out on their puffas for a while until the water was deep enough for them to stand up and hide their expansive crotches. They waded out a bit further and turned back to see if they could locate their girlfriends somewhere on the beach. After a quick scan, Perry saw the girls walking up towards the beach bar.

'Which one's my one, Kevin?' he asked, not really sure what the protocol was for deciding who got who in a two-boys/two-girls type situation.

'The fat one,' said Kevin without missing a beat, figuring that since Perry was on the chunky side himself, he'd prefer a girl with a bit of blubber on her.

'Oh thanks, Kev,' replied Perry, grateful he'd got the one he fancied. 'I love my fat one. She understands me.'

'You haven't even talked to her yet,' replied Kevin, who, although he indulged in moments of mutual fantasy with Perry, thought it a bit much to say this girl — who had never even looked at Perry — 'understood' him. Perry nodded, acknowledging this basic and rather obvious truth.

Stiffies now cooled and retreated, the boys waded back towards shore, their puffas so filled with water that when they stepped onto the beach the jackets looked like huge bags of black jelly, gushing and splashing water on irritated sunbathers as they made their way to the bar.

The girls – who had seated themselves at a small table by the time Kevin and Perry appeared – fell silent as the two boys tried to adopt cosmopolitan, enigmatic poses off to one side. Unfortunately, their jackets made it difficult to look anything other than a couple of sad twits who'd gone swimming with their clothes on, and the boys – realizing they might not look as 100 per cent cool as they'd have liked – quietly slid out of them and let them fall with a squelchy thud to the floor. Kevin looked at his jacket as if he could not possibly imagine how this big black bag of gunk had managed to wrap itself around his shoulders. He tutted knowingly, and Perry responded by dumping his own jacket and kicking it away with as much disdain as he could muster.

The girls ignored them.

Unsure whether this was because the girls hadn't seen them, they were playing hard to get or they simply didn't like them, Kevin and Perry sat down in the chairs opposite. 'Afternoon ladies,' said Kevin, in a strangulated voice – which he thought made him sound like Pierce Brosnan in *The World Is Not Enough* but actually sounded closer to Dick Van Dyke in *Mary Poppins*.

'Howzit hangin', ladies?' added Perry, in a voice which had the double disadvantage of trying to sound like Kevin trying to sound like Pierce Brosnan.

The girls ignored them.

'Certainly a lovely day afternoon for the beach, eh ladies?' offered Kevin, certain that any minute now they would take a bite on his conversational bait. They didn't. Instead, the slightly miserable-looking one picked up her mobile from the table and punched a number in a blur of fingers and chipped nail polish.

'Yeah, 's me' she said, keeping her eyes firmly fixed on her chubby friend. 'Cos maybe we're going to El Divino tonight, yeah?'

Perry, who thought he should make an effort to get to know his girlfriend better, spoke up. 'Would you ladies like a drink?' She ignored him and continued staring at her friend on the phone.

'Or Pasha, yeah' continued her mate, who took the phone away from her ear and turned to Perry. 'I only drink margarita with no salt, innit Gemma?' She nodded to her friend.

Gemma, the chubby one, nodded back at the girl on the phone. 'It is Candice, and me.'

Introductions complete, Candice returned to her phone call. 'Cos Ministry's at Pasha innit yeah?'

A waiter walked past and Kevin managed to get his attention with a self-conscious wave of his arm. 'Two margaritas with no salt please waiter, shaken not stirred,' he said, convinced – now that the girls had told them their names – that they were in there.

'...or Manumission...' continued Candice.

Kevin suddenly realized Candice was talking about where the girls were going to go out that night. For the life of him, he couldn't remember any other clubs, but thought it might give the game away if he took out his soggy copy of *Mixmag* and started looking them up. 'Yeah, we might go to Manumission tonight, eh Perry?' suggested Kevin, in an attempt to sound knowledgeable.

'Yeah...' said Perry, only just beginning to twig what was going on.

'Or Es Paradis or Privilege or Amnesia,' continued Candice, who didn't really know what she was talking about either, but she had a good memory for names and had read the clubber's guide in her hotel room before coming to the beach.

'Or Es Paradis or Privilege or Amnesia heh, Perry,' repeated Kevin.

'Yeah...' added Perry, whose brain couldn't keep up with the pace of conversation.

Candice continued. 'Yeah, cos the choons at Amnesia are bangin'...' Halfway though her sentence the phone gave out a shrill ring and in horror she slammed it on the table, unanswered. The girls stared at each other, blushing furiously, their embarrassment tempered only by the arrival of the waiter who brought two margaritas and put them on the table. Kevin paid with a flourish of a banknote, and an offer for the waiter to keep the change. Since this worked out at about fifteen pence, all he got was a sneer for his effort.

The girls, crimson-faced, downed the drinks in one sloppy gulp, jumped up out of the chairs and, without saying a word, scuttled away down the beach.

'They're very lovely ladies, aren't they Kev?' said Perry, thinking he might be falling in love.

'Yeah, very lovely ladies,' agreed Kev.

'What's my chubby babe called again?'

'Gemma,' said Kev. 'And mine's Candice.'

'Gemma's got such a lovely personality,' said Perry wistfully.

'Candice is *so kind* and interesting...'

Their musing were rudely interrupted by the mobile, left on the table by the girls, which burst into life again. It rang for ages whilst the boys looked at each other, paralysed by indecision, until Perry cautiously picked it up.

'Hello...?' he said. Kevin heard a woman's voice yattering away in Perry's ear. 'Er, yeah,' said Perry. 'I'll just get her.' He stood up to see where the girls had gone and found them crouching miserably near the sea. Kevin – realizing his mate would no more shout for them than drop his trousers and get his willy out for the waiter – decided to yell on his behalf. 'Ladies!' he bellowed, pointing at Perry who was holding the phone. The girls ignored them, and so they left the bar and scooted down the beach.

When they got to the girls Perry shoved the phone under Candice's nose. 'It's your mummy...' he said. Candice, horrified, grabbed it out of Perry's hand and together the girls leapt up and stormed away up the beach, Candice screaming abuse at her mother down the phone.

The boys stood and watched them disappear into the distance.

'They love us...' said Perry.

'Yup,' said Kevin, convinced he almost had a girl-friend.

# chapter seven

The streets bustled with clubbers, street artists, mime-artists, nutters in weird flouncy costumes, jugglers on stilts, fire-breathers — everything from monsta-cool ravers to scary super-freaks.

The boys wandered aimlessly through the streets, taking in the sights, sounds and smells, and trying to look as cool as possible. Sunbathing opportunities aside, the transformation that the island had undertaken from day to night could not have been more dramatic, and the boys were overawed with the sheer energy of it all. They were real teenagers now, equals amongst revellers. It felt dangerous, exciting, and most important of all — incredibly grown-up.

Perry had brought his digital camcorder with him — the one he'd got with his reward money — and was doing a Nick Broomfield-style exposé on the nightlife. This basically meant recording everything he saw and talking bollocks over the top of it. 'The evening begins,' he commentated, waving the camera around in an attempt to copy funky yoof TV angles. 'And superstar DJs Kev P. and Perr E. hit the town...'

'Pel! Over there!' Kevin's hand swung into vision through the viewfinder and Perry followed the line of his arm until — miracle of miracles! — he framed Candice and Gemma, sitting with their backs to the boys in an open-fronted bar.

'Whoah, and there are our girlfriends Candice and Gemma, whom we love…' continued Perry's voice-over. Perry did a crash zoom on the girls, only to reveal that as they stood up to leave the bar, it wasn't Candice or Gemma at all – just a couple of girls who looked like them. 'Aw…' he said, genuinely disappointed.

'Just another pretty girl and her fat mate,' said Kevin's disembodied voice off-camera, making no effort to disguise the fact that he thought he had a better-looking girlfriend than Perry. The little dig was lost on Perry, who turned the camera off and decided to look at Ibiza without one of his eyes closed for a while.

'How come all pretty girls have a fat mate?' he asked, still not quite understanding what Kevin was getting at.

'It's the law,' replied Kevin. As if to prove the point, a pretty girl and a fat girl walked past them chattering to themselves, oblivious to the fact they'd just proved a dubious theory correct. Perry was about to film them when something in the crowd alarmed him so much he stopped dead in his tracks.

'Kevin. What the bloody hell's that?' Further down the crowded street they saw five overly suntanned men with seriously naff mullet haircuts, moustaches, and Eighties-style short-sleeved shirts loping towards them in single file.

'Germans,' replied Kevin ominously as the Teutonic crocodile wove past them and headed on up the road. Perry quickly raised the camera and captured them for posterity.

They drifted randomly through the streets for hours: watching, filming and mucking about. This was so much fun. Perry was about to video a bloke dressed up like a suitcase when Kevin jumped in front of the camera and licked his lips in a way that he hoped looked seductive (but actually looked like he had a cold sore) and whispered, 'Candice... suck my candy.'

Perry sniggered, then turned the camera on himself. 'Gemma!... Lick my love plank,' he said in the sexiest voice he could manage. He turned the camera back on Kevin, who'd put on this silly, rapturous expression. It didn't stay rapturous for very long. Kevin recoiled in horror at something behind Perry. Perry swung around to find his viewfinder filled with the sheepish face of Kevin's dad. No wonder he looked sheepish. He'd just finished giving (a very raunchy-looking) Mrs Patterson an enormous snog. Mrs Patterson? Snogging? Perry squirmed as he realised that on an island full of luscious, gorgeous, sexy women, the one who gave him the biggest stiffy of all was his best mate's mum.

Oh dear.

If Kevin had paid attention in his English classes (which of course he hadn't) he'd have known that right now he was stuck in Dante's fifth circle of hell – Having Dinner With Your Parents On Holiday. It was beyond dreadful. The restaurant – all checked table cloths and breadstick holders – was full of old couples in smart (i.e. crappy) clothes and drinking wine in half bottles in case they got tipsy. The Gypsy Kings were playing in the background – music that was so appallingly bad it almost had Kevin gagging. And as for the place itself – he was just glad it was indoors so no one even remotely worthy would see him in there with all these old farts.

They all sat around a table, romantically lit by a single candle in an old wicker wine bottle: Mr Patterson strumming an air banjo and Mrs Patterson smiling contentedly on one side, Kevin and Perry — not so relaxed and cheerful — on the other. Kevin had descended into a major sulk whilst Perry, as usual, had his standard, uncomfortably lost look about him.

Mr Patterson was the first to break the silence. 'Well...isn't this fun!' he said trying to arouse some enthusiasm in the boys. Kevin looked over at Perry and rolled his eyes.

'What would you boys like to eat?' asked Mrs Patterson, desperately trying to inject some excitement into the proceedings and avert the coming storm.

'I'm NOT HUNGRY,' huffed Kevin.

'Come on son, you must eat something,' chirped his dad. 'You'll need the energy if you want to go bopping in a disco.'

*Bopping in a disco?* Kevin recoiled in disgust. His father was such an embarrassment he could barely stand to be in the same room as him.

A waiter appeared at the table behind Mr Patterson. 'Señor?' he asked. Mr Patterson grabbed the menu — glad of the diversion — and scanned the plastic-covered pages.

'We'll order for everybody, shall we?' he suggested. Mrs Patterson agreed. 'Como el primer plato quisiera tapas una mezcla, por favor,' he continued, feeling quite proud of the fact he'd remembered so much Spanish from the course he'd taken at work years back. Kevin moaned as humiliation heaped upon humiliation. His father — trying to speak their stupid lingo — what a complete horror. Then — to pile on the misery even further — his mother joined in.

'Y despues una gran paella por todo,' she added with a smile. Kevin groaned and put his head in his hands. Perry groaned as well, but for altogether different reasons. Mrs Patterson speaking Spanish was possibly the horniest thing he'd ever heard. Truly, genuinely, awe-inspiringly pantie-tastic.

'Gran paella, cara mia?' said Mr Patterson to his wife, quite enjoying himself now.

'Si si,' she replied, with a twinkle in her eye. 'Una necita se fuerte para hacer el amor, cara mia...' She ran her fingers down his face and smiled sexily. Perry had no idea Mrs Patterson had just said Mr P. would need strength for lovemaking – but then he didn't have to. He got the gist of it loud and clear. And so did Kevin, who started retching loudly and attracting disapproving glares from the other diners.

Perry didn't care about the other diners. He had other problems on his hands. Or rather, in his lap.

'That's strange,' said Mr Patterson. 'This table's gone a bit wobbly.' Perry whimpered as his glass fell over and rolled slowly away from him. Yes, thought Mr Patterson to himself, it's definitely higher over on Perry's side. He gave it a firm shake, making Perry squeak and go an odd shade of purple. 'We need a wedge,' he decided after giving the table another good rattle. 'Pass me that beer mat, sexypants...'

'Oh for God's sake!' exploded Kevin, unable to take any more of this drippy affection between his parents. He leapt to his feet and, with a theatrical swing of his long arms, huffed away. Perry – caught once more between his best mate and his best mate's mum and dad – pushed his chair back from the table to leave. It promptly slammed down level.

'Mr, Mrs Patterson,' he mumbled and scurried away, bent double, leaving Kevin's parents staring in mute astonishment.

Back on the streets, Perry caught up with Kevin, who was striding away from the restaurant in a major strop.

'What a couple of wankers!' snapped Kevin.

'Yeah, we are int we...' agreed Perry.

'No!' yelled Kevin in disgust at Perry's misunder-standing. 'My parents!'

'Oh yeah, sorry' said Perry, still not quite seeing what Mr and Mrs Patterson had done to get Kevin riled up. It was all so confusing sometimes. Perry didn't fight with his mum – not much anyway – and he hardly saw his dad these days so there wasn't really much chance for arguing. Of course, if Kevin said Mr and Mrs P. were being a couple of wankers, then it stood to reason they *were* being a couple of wankers. Perry just didn't see how, or why. It was something he had to trust Kevin on.

They turned a corner, the delights of the Ibizan nightlife slightly tarnished by the scene in the restaurant, only to find themselves smack bang outside the most famous club of all, the holy Mecca of rave, the Vatican City of largin' it. *Amnesia!*

It was enormous. Lit from all angles by coloured floods and twisting lasers, it stood in front of them like some clubbing cathedral. A long fat queue of would-be ravers wove its way from the entrance and down the street, with groups of people hanging around in clumps waiting to meet friends or just watching the club in eager awe. 'Cool!' mumbled Kevin, completely blown away.

'Rinsin'!' stuttered Perry.

'Large!' shouted Kevin.

As they stood dwarfed by the building (and what it represented), a familiar white limousine pulled up right outside the club, and its door opened. Out stepped their new best mate ever, Eye Ball Paul. The driver dashed round the back and started unloading the record cases.

'Come on Big Baz! Shift, you fat tart,' said Eye Ball Paul, checking his reflection in the shaded windows of the limo. The driver gave the DJ a look that would have got him sacked if Eye Ball Paul wasn't so wrapped up in himself that he failed to notice it. The boys strode across the road and planted themselves next to the DJ, who had his back to them watching Muff and Wankette struggle out of the back seat.

'Alright, Eye Ball Paul' said Kevin. The DJ turned round.

'It's the little wankers from the airport!' Result! Eye Ball Paul liked to have a monkey or two around to take the shit, and his long-time driver and whipping boy, Big Baz, was proving too unsatisfactorily lippy these days to be genuinely good fun. And what did he have here, served on a plate with a double helping of fries and a side order of onion rings? Why, two perfectly abusable new monkey-boys.

'You doin' a set here tonight, Eye Ball Paul?' asked the tragic ginger kid.

'How's your mummy, Ginger Pubes?' said Eye Ball Paul, determined to get as many insults in as he could. The fat short one laughed.

'Hur Hur...' sniggered the tragic ginger kid. 'She's a bitch! Hur!'

Eye Ball Paul nodded in the direction of Big Baz, who was struggling to get the records out of the car. 'Don't just stand there Ginger Pubes. Give him a hand.' The kid looked overjoyed at being given some menial labouring, and scuttled round to take one of the boxes off Big Baz's hands. The dopey-looking one stayed where he was. 'And you, Sad Act!' ordered Eye Ball Paul. The kid didn't laugh so much at his own nickname, the DJ thought satisfactorily to himself as he went to help his friend. It might even hurt his feelings. I'll have to remember that one.

The boys took a heavy case each, and followed the DJ, Big Baz and the girls into the club through a side entrance. That meant walking the entire length of the queue with everyone watching. The lads couldn't have felt more important if they'd had Kate Moss running after them begging for an autograph and a swifty behind the drinks crates out back. To make matters even better, they saw Candice and Gemma standing desolately in the line of clubbers.

'Ladies,' called Kevin importantly as they walked past.

'Ladies,' added Perry, somewhat unnecessarily.

The girls saw them and said nothing.

The lads weren't just inside Amnesia. They were *back-stage* at Amnesia. This was like getting a glimpse of a girl's growler when sunbathing in the park – unexpected but thoroughly welcome. Eye Ball Paul's entourage (of which they were now surely members) was being led through a maze of black-painted corridors by the club's ushers. Despite their arms feeling like they were going to be ripped out of their sockets by the record cases, Kevin and Perry were ecstatic.

'Er... Eye Ball Paul?' ventured Kevin.

'What the fuck do you want?' snapped the DJ, who was none too happy about his monkey-boys getting mouthy on him.

'Hur...um... We done some mixes of our own...' said Kevin.

'What? You and Sad Act?' asked Eye Ball Paul, climbing the stairs at a pace only someone without half a ton of records at the end of each arm could manage.

'Yeah, me and Sad Act,' replied Kevin. Perry winced. He didn't like the nickname Sad Act, and was a little hurt that Kevin should use it. But Kevin didn't seem to notice. He was too busy sucking up to Eye Ball Paul. 'I don't suppose we could play them to you sometime could we perhaps please thank you no alright then?'

'So you're brother DJs yeah?' asked Eye Ball Paul, clearly not interested.

'Er...yeah.' Suddenly Eye Ball Paul and the entire crew stopped and turned back to the boys, who shrank beneath their interrogative stares. Here was some sport, thought the DJ to himself.

'So what's your collection? What choons you got? What beats you into?' Kevin gulped. He wasn't quite sure what beats he was into. Everything cool really. But that clearly wasn't the response Eye Ball Paul was looking for. A mistake here could prove costly. 'House or Garage?' asked the DJ, getting impatient.

Multiple choice. Kevin understood that. At least I've got a chance here, he thought to himself. 50/50. He just wished there was an audience he could ask.

'Um... House?' Eye Ball Paul and the crew relaxed and nodded. House was clearly the right answer. But they turned on him again, more aggressively than before.

'Acid House, or Pumping House?' demanded the DJ.

'Erm...Pumping House...' plucked Kevin from thin air.

Eye Ball Paul nodded. 'Balearic Pumpin' or Commercial Pumpin'?' Kevin felt on safer ground here. He'd read an article about Eye Ball Paul and he remembered seeing the word Balearic. He didn't know what it meant of course, but he *had* seen it.

'Balearic...' he said, with a little confidence.

Eye Ball Paul looked almost pleased. But then he played his joker. 'Sash or Chicane?' he demanded.

'Er... Sash!' replied Kevin, thinking he was in the safety zone by now. No such luck. Eye Ball Paul and the crew erupted into spiteful arrogant laughter.

'Boys!' snorted the DJ. 'These blaggers are PANTS!' The crew laughed louder and Kevin and Perry tried to join in, not sure if they were in on the joke, or the butt of it. Eye Ball Paul wiped a tear from his cheek, and still laughing, thrust a business card into Kevin's sweaty hand. 'Yeah, I'll hear your mix.' He said this to the crew, not the boys, obviously still taking the piss. 'My pad. Tomorrow. Be there.' And with that, he disappeared through a doorway into the DJ booth, leaving the boys standing open-mouthed on the staircase, unable to comprehend their enormous good luck. Eye Ball Paul's head reappeared through the doorway. 'Now... FUCK OFF!' he shouted at them.

Kevin and Perry dropped the cases and legged it back down the stairs, giving Eye Ball Paul and his crew a big thumbs up as they went, the sound of the entourage's laughter swallowed by the thumping beat from the club as they headed back down the corridor. 'Thanks, Eye Ball Paul,' said Kevin.

'Thank you,' added Perry. He turned to Kevin. 'He is such a nice bloke!'

'Brilliant,' replied Kevin. 'We're gonna be DJs!'


Outside in the queue, things weren't quite so brilliant for Candice and Gemma. After standing in line for nearly an hour they got within sight of the front entrance only to find themselves dragged out of the queue by a little weaselly man in a white shirt and a black bow tie. He had a thin moustache and greased-back hair and was clearly a bouncer, but not the knuckled-headed sort that usually stood at the front entrance to night-clubs. There was a malicious, nasty look about him that made both the girls recoil.

'Sorry, girls,' he slimed at them. 'No monsters.' He waved his arm and a new batch of beautiful ravers walked past him and up to the pay desk. 'Beautiful people can pass, but monsters, no.'

Gemma looked at Candice in despair. What was this bloke trying to say? The bouncer obviously understood the look and repeated himself. 'Do you understand? Beauties...' he pointed to three girls going past him, '... yes! Monsters...no! Look.' He took out a vanity mirror from his top pocket and held it up to the girls' faces. 'Your faces', he punched the mirror from behind and it shattered into small pieces which he gently dropped, tinkling, to the ground, 'offend my mirror. Do you see what I'm saying?'

The girls saw what he was saying all too clearly. Without another word they turned and clattered away from the club, arms linked and eyes filling with tears.

'Cos I didn't wanna go anyway,' said Candice, as much for her benefit as for Gemma's.

'Yeah, me neither,' said Gemma. They scurried away in silence, careful not to let anyone see them crying.

'And maybe tomorrow,' said Candice after a while, 'I'm gonna have a makeover wiv Boots beauty products innit.'

'...Yeah and me...'

'And them boys can get us in tomorrow cos they're mates wiv Eye Ball Paul, innit.'

'Yeah, best mates,' said Gemma. What an excellent idea. Boots beauty products and two boys who could get them into the club.

It was all gonna be alright.

They might lose their virginity yet.


On their way out of the club, through labyrinthine tunnels and corridors, the boys took a wrong turn and found themselves hopelessly lost. They didn't want to ask directions from any of the backstage crew who were knocking around. Despite being part of Eye Ball

Paul's entourage (well, almost anyway) they both had a sneaky suspicion they could get thrown out if they looked as if they didn't know where they were going. So they just kept wandering. Problem was, it all looked the same – black walls and manky, sticky carpet (years of spilled beers, stubbed-out fags and vomiting groupies had given the floor covering that unique, sought-after venue look). After ten minutes of semi-adventurous rambling they came across a door that seemed to be thumping on its hinges with the noise coming from the other side. The boys looked at each other, grinned, and tugged it open.

Amnesia hit them in the face like an audio sledge-hammer.

No amount of late night TV shows on the club scene had prepared them for this. First was the noise, less a sound than a rhythmic punch in the guts by a pissed-off Mike Tyson, accompanied by a similar ripping-off-of-ears. Then there was the lights. If you didn't suffer from epilepsy before you went into Amnesia, you could put good money on suffering from it by the time you came out. It reminded Perry of the brainwashing scene in this old film where they strapped Michael Caine (the spy Harry Palmer!) into a chair and played weird music to him VERY VERY LOUD whilst shining all these lights in his face. And then...the people. Short of actually having them stand on each others' shoulders, you couldn't have crammed more into the club. Any flat, reasonably strong surface – chair, table, shelf, counter – had someone standing up and dancing on it. And in cages around the club were these beautiful girls dancing in a way that had them both twitching in their underpants.

This was awesome. This was Amnesia. This was *rinsin'!*

73

# chapter eight

'Oh man, that was bangin'!' said Perry as the boys ambled along the roadside.

'Eye Ball Paul plays hammerin' choons,' replied Kevin, who was trying to walk and dance at the same time, their classy moves from the night before including 'Big Fish Little Fish', 'Stacking Shelves' and (Perry's favourite) 'Makin' Boxes'.

It was that peculiar hour of dawn when the last of the bars were closing and the first of the breakfast cafes opening, the smells of the Ibizan national dish (sausage, egg, chips and beans) gently interwoven between the odours of stale beer and pavement pizza. The closely-packed bars and cafes gradually fell away as they neared home, the edge of the sea crimson with the dawn sun, the sky still glittering with the last of the Mediterranean stars. It was truly beautiful – but since it had neither pointy nipples nor long legs it was the sort of beauty that largely passed Kevin and Perry by.

'Hey, what happened to our lovely ladies?' asked Perry as the apartment came into sight.

'Maybe they didn't get in,' replied Kevin, who had secretly spent most of the night scanning the faces in the club for Gemma so he could 'accidentally' bump into her. 'You gotta be sorted to get into a club like that.'

Kevin wasn't quite sure what constituted 'sorted' but he knew it had something to do with that elusive 'cool' factor that most eighteen-year-olds had, and most fifteen-year-olds didn't.

'Well we'll get 'em in, won't we Kev, cos we're gonna be loved-up DJs.' Once again Perry's interpretation of the world skated dangerously on the thin ice of fantasy — and as usual he was deaf to the sound of it creaking ominously beneath the weight of reality.

'We're havin' it large!' said Kevin enthusiastically.

'We've been up all night, Kev!' added Perry, impressed at his staying power. By now the lads had reached the stairs by the side of their apartment and they began climbing them, still making boxes and still stacking them.

'We bleached it!' said Kevin, opening the door to the chalet.

'Bleached it,' added Perry stepping in. 'Here, if we get the girls in tomorrow, we'll be up all night shagging… urg!' Perry skidded to a halt and emitted a herniated whelp. Kevin froze, and felt his bowels loosen.

Grown-ups. Naked. On the sofa. Perry's squawk woke them and in a flurry of cushions and discarded clothing they managed to cover themselves in less time than it takes to trigger an H-bomb.

'Hello, Perry,' said Mrs Patterson trying to sound light, breezy and normal. She patted down her hair and smiled weakly.

'Perry…' said Mr P., clutching a cushion to his groin and looking as casual as he could.

'Mr, Mrs Patterson, hur hur hur!' sniggered Perry. This was too good to be true. He'd just seen Mrs Patterson's tits. Not through a blouse or a swimming costume, but real life in the flesh proper in-yer-face tits. And she'd been doing it with Mr Patterson. Doing it!

That meant she was still up for it, even though she was a mum. Perry wouldn't have believed it if he hadn't seen it for himself. That meant maybe...just maybe... she was nice to him because...what? She fancied him? Could that be it? Could Mrs Patterson be up for it with Perry like that woman in *The Graduate* was up for it with Dustin Hoffman? What an amazing thought. *What a horny thought*!

'Hello, darling,' said Mrs Patterson, turning to Kevin, thankfully oblivious to what was happening in both Perry's head and his trousers. 'Had a good night?' It was all she could think of to say in the circumstances.

Kevin looked at his parents with bile in his throat. He could not be more disgusted if he'd found cat shit in his cornflakes. Actually, cat shit in his cornflakes would be preferable. Apart from seeing his parents'...things, it was fairly obvious that they'd been...been...urrgh, he couldn't bring himself to think of it. It was just too repulsive. 'You are disgusting...!' he stammered, too shocked to even shout. He stumbled away to his room and slammed the door behind him. Perry — as always — followed three steps behind, but as he opened the door to join Kevin he turned to Kevin's mum and gave her a big wink. Yeah, she was up for it alright. Definitely. There's every chance, thought Perry, that I might lose my virginity to Mrs Patterson. Wow...

Perry — mind in a spin — went into the bedroom and sat next to Kevin, who was on the edge of the bed with his head in his hands, clearly upset about something. Perry tried to cheer him up. 'Your mum and dad were doin' it Kev!' Any talk of sex usually cheered Kevin up no end, and Perry thought this was as perfect a conversation piece as you could wish for.

'Shut up, Perry!' snapped Kevin. 'That is disgusting! They do not do it. They've only ever done it once.' And in his mind, Kevin was convinced this was the truth. Anyone with a brain knew that once people got out of their twenties, they stopped having sex. It would be too putrid. The idea of saggy tits and beer guts wobbling away beneath the covers was the kind of stuff perverts thought about. But his parents – obviously, because they were his parents – would never have enjoyed sex. It would have been as repugnant for them to do it as it was for Kevin to think about it. As his parents, they had a duty to be non-sexual. It was an issue Kevin had wrestled with since realizing what sex was all about and he'd worked out how he'd come to be conceived. The scenario in his head was the only possible answer. It had to be.

It worked like this. Option One – he was adopted. A very attractive choice, especially given how shitty his parents were to him most of the time. This also offered the romantic possibilities of having parents somewhere who abandoned him because: (i) they were Russian dissidents fleeing Communist oppression during the Eighties and had to give up their baby for his own safety; (ii) his mother was a famous model who had to give him away because her top modelling career dictated that she wasn't allowed to have children, especially by mega-famous rock stars; or (iii) he was the illegitimate son of a world-leading politician whose existence could spark the collapse of several Western governments and lead to him being secretly ushered in as the dictator head of a new European super-state. These were all very possible (and attractive) scenarios. Problem is, Kevin (aged ten) bore such a striking resemblance to his dad (photographs of him aged eleven) that they could be the same bloke. And Kevin and his mum shared identical snail-shaped birthmarks on their shoulder blades, so genetically speaking, there was no doubt who his parents were. Disappointing as it may be, he was not adopted.

Option Two – his parents had never had sex, and he was a test-tube baby. This idea just didn't feel right – it had no glamour, no mystery, and why the medical community would waste all that time and effort on such an evidently boring couple as his mum and dad defied explanation, even though he, Kevin, was the product. Somehow it didn't add up.

Option Three – they'd had sex, but only once, in order to make him. This was clearly the way things happened. In Kevin's mind, the night it happened his parents had been lying side by side in bed, both ashen-faced at the task that lay before them. 'I'm sorry darling, but I'm afraid we're going to have to do it,' his dad had no doubt murmured. 'Us? Do it? What a revolting thought,' his mother had replied, probably gagging a bit. 'I know,' his dad continued, 'but it's the only way if you're to give birth to the world's greatest DJ mixmaster genius…' His mother no doubt winced at the awful duty she had to undertake to create her boy genius. 'You're right,' she would have said, distressed. 'I'll turn out the light and close my eyes…' Kevin couldn't bring himself to imagine the next two or three seconds, but there was probably a cry or two of disgust from each of them and the lights would immediately have come back on again.

'Thank God that's over,' his mum would have said.

'Yup, never again,' his dad would have replied. And then…then their self-loathing would have got the better of them, and they'd both have vomited into the bowls they had put aside for this moment, the sensation of being sick infinitely better than the gross act they'd just had to commit. Yeah, that was definitely the only way to describe it.

'What's up, Kev?' came Perry's voice, thankfully breaking Kevin's awful reverie.

'I just had a revolting thought,' said Kevin shuddering. Perry, of course, had not been having revolting thoughts at all. Quite the opposite. Lying on the bed, staring at the ceiling, he'd just been replaying in his mind the moment when he'd stepped through the door and caught Mrs P. without her kit on. He hadn't quite got a view of her...thingie, but her tits. Whoah! They were fantastic!

As if to mirror what was happening in his head, strange sounds started coming from Mr and Mrs Patterson's bedroom next door. Rhythmic creaking. Giggling. Faster rhythmic creaking. More giggling. Voices, laughter. Perry grinned. They were doing it again! Mr and Mrs Patterson were *shagging!* Unbelievable! Perry turned to Kevin to give him the thumbs-up, but Kevin was lying back on the bed grimacing as if he was in a great deal of pain. There was a particularly loud burst of giggling and Kevin stuck his fingers in his ears and started humming to himself, his pained expression even worse.

'We'll be doing that with Candice and Gemma, won't we, Kev!' said Perry, completely oblivious to Kevin's vast discomfort at hearing his parents banging away like a couple of rabbits. Kevin hummed louder to himself, now deeply in denial. 'Won't we, Kev?' continued Perry, as the creaking got louder and louder. 'Won't we, Kev?' he repeated, frustrated that Kevin was ignoring him, 'Won't we, Kev?'

'Doing *what?*' shouted Kevin, wishing Perry would just shut up.

'We'll be at it! Shagging! Like your parents!'

'Perry! They are not shagging!' Kevin was in danger of going completely mad. One half of his brain told him that he could hear his parents shagging. Very clearly, and very unambiguously. But the other half of his brain told him his parents did not shag, ever. Couldn't shag. *Wouldn't* shag. The two halves fought for supremacy. Kevin was dizzy, caught in a looped mental maelstrom.

By now the evidence was overwhelming. The creaking had become a frenetic pounding, and above the groaning and thumping could be heard Mrs Patterson's voice, very distinct and very animated, crying out Ray's name over and over again. Faster and faster. Louder and louder. Moans, groans, cries, shouts...

It was all too much for Kevin. With a scream of pain and revulsion, he threw his bedclothes over his head and tried to stop the noise from getting into his ears. If he couldn't hear it, it wasn't happening, so he buried his head under the pillow and squeezed it tightly around his ears.

*parents shagging parents shagging parents shagging parents shagging*

But it was happening. Right here, right now. *Oh God what terrible torture...*

By now, Perry had completely tuned Kevin out. He lay back, an innocent smile on his face, and a tent pole of a stiffy holding up his bedspread. After a couple of particularly loud moans from next door, the sound stopped. Kevin, grateful it was all over, pulled his pillow over his head and tried to pretend it had never happened.

Perry, on the other hand, pulled his jeans up, and went for a mysteriously long trip to the bathroom.

It was some time before either of them got to sleep.

Mr and Mrs Patterson pottered around the kitchen in their kimonos, brewing coffee, making toast and singing Oasis's 'Wonderwall' badly to each other, more Dean Martin than Liam Gallagher.

Mr Patterson ran his fingers through his wife's hair as she sat sipping her coffee and reading the tour guide book they'd picked up at the airport. This was certainly turning into a fine holiday. They hadn't been this...erm, 'energetic' since before Kevin was born, and even then Ray didn't think he'd had as much staying power as this. He felt very pleased with himself. It must be the sea air, the warm weather and the safe knowledge that Kevin and his pal were intent on spending every minute of the holiday as far away from the oldies as possible, which suited Ray down to the ground. Even so, it was a bit silly of them to fall asleep on the sofa like that, especially considering where his head had been when he'd dozed off. Oh well, never mind. Kevin was old enough to know what went on between grown-ups. In fact, Ray wouldn't have been that surprised if Kevin and Perry didn't have their own little holiday romances brewing. Mind you, the thought of Kevin actually...*doing it* with a girl was almost too much for Ray to think about. Never mind almost, it *was* too much to think about. Gross and disgusting actually.

Thankfully, the sound of his wife singing the chorus shattered the rather unpleasant image that had been forming in Ray's head.

Just then the door to Kevin's bedroom burst open and he stomped into the room with an expression of pure thunder on his face, knocking back the last of a can of Coke. Perry – surprise, surprise – was a few steps behind.

'Never *ever* sing that again!' Kevin retorted, for no apparent reason. Ray frowned. What now? God, it was like walking on eggshells with the boy around. Everything you said or did just seemed to turn him into this furious monster.

'But we like Oasis, Kevin,' said Ray, slightly confused.

'You do not like Oasis,' shouted Kevin, trying to claim some territorial stake over his music, music that old people weren't even allowed to know about, let alone 'sing'. 'You're all saggy and rotted. You've never even heard of Oasis!' Kevin was seething. He'd had the most disturbing dreams about his parents doing it, and then had woken up to realize it was all true. They were trying to be young, like him. They weren't young. They were old and they were nearly dead. And now having them sing his music was throwing him into paroxysms of bewilderment. They were parents, for God's sake. They should listen to Frank Sinatra or something. And they should never, ever do it. Ever. It was disgusting. With that final thought he lobbed the empty can towards the bin, missing its target the can fell onto the stone floor with a noisy clatter.

'Pick it up, darling,' said his mum imploringly.

'I AM NOT YOUR SLAVE!' bellowed Kevin, yanking open the front door and disappearing down the steps outside in an avalanche of trainers. Mrs Patterson turned to her husband and shook her head in bemusement.

She turned to Perry and gained some comfort from the fact that Perry wasn't as volatile as her own son. She wondered for a moment if Kevin was as quiet and polite to Perry's mum as Perry was to her when he came over. 'What's up with Prince Charming?' she enquired, thinking maybe Perry might be able to offer some insight into Kevin's third tantrum of the holiday. Instead, Perry just gave her this weird stare and winked again at her, quite lasciviously if the truth be told.

'Mrs Patterson,' he said, grabbing hold of his crotch and scuttling away in a lumpy 'Perry' sort of way. He disappeared out the door and once again the Pattersons were left on their own.

Ray shrugged. On his wife's advice, he'd given up getting stroppy, and look how much happier he was for it! Bugger those boys, he thought to himself, pouring some champagne into his wife's orange juice. They can do what they like. I'm having a *great* time. He leant over and kissed her neck. 'Bucks Fizz, Mrs Five Times?'

She smiled and reached inside his kimono. She doubted he had the energy to make her Mrs Six Times. Could be fun trying, though.

# chapter nine

Big Baz, Eye Ball Paul's driver, odd-job man and general kick-about, dunked the sponge into the bucket of soapy water and slapped it onto the bonnet of the limo, splashing suds liberally across the car, the road and his legs. The motor didn't really need another wash – it only ever got taken out to go to and from the club when the guv'nor was doing a gig – but Baz thought he'd rather be outside working on the car than sitting inside having to listen to his dickhead employer going on about what a fantastic DJ he was, how rinsin' and cool and large and over-fucking-whelmingly brilliant.

It wasn't always like this. A few years back, before Eye Ball got famous, he'd actually been an alright geezer to work for. A bit up himself, but then most of these DJ blokes were. Except Norman, of course. A real gent he was, dead quiet and all that, but nice with it. No, Eye Ball hadn't been too bad really, a right laugh sometimes. But then he'd had that hit single a couple of seasons ago – 'Spunky Munky Minky Spinky' – and from then on he'd just crawled further and further up his own arse. Stardom did that to you – that, the booze and the drugs. And the tarts. Jeez, there'd been bloody thousands of them – brainless little dolly birds who'd sooner open their legs than

start a conversation. And the effec... of ...
feeble-minded Eye Ball Paul (or Paul R... ...
really was, and hated being called) was ... ... turn b...
into a class-A, bona fide, certified knob-end. ...

First, he'd lost his sense of humour — or a... ...
allowed it to descend into cruel piss-taking, which was
kind of worse really because it always meant he was on
the look-out for victims. The tiny glimpse of stardom
he'd got gave him the idea he could treat people like
shit. Then he'd surrounded himself with all these
hangers-on and arse-lickers who didn't have the nerve
to tell him when he was being a twat. For someone who
had the capacity to be an enormously twatty king of
twats when he wanted, this was not good. When you
got a bit of fame, you needed people around you who
would bring you back down to earth a bit, not put you
on a pedestal, laugh at every piss-poor joke you made
and pretend they were your mates.

But Big Baz was no idiot, and he knew a good deal
when he saw one. All he had to do was drive the DJ
superstar around when he was told to, lug records
around when he had to, smile nicely and take all the
flak the prat threw at him. He got to spend the summer
in the sun, the winter in the best hotels and clubs back
home, and got shed-loads of freebies in the process. All
in all, not a bad little earner for a bloke who left school
with a GCSE in metalwork and had spent most of the
time since then doing crappy jobs for crappy money in
crappy weather. The one constant in it all was the
crappy employers. Fuck 'em, thought Baz to himself,
picking up the hose and spraying the car with clean
water. I'm alright, me. They can all go stuff themselves.

Baz took a chamois leather out of the back of his
shorts and started wiping the car dry. As he leant over
to do the roof, he saw the two lads from the airport

walking towards him on the other side of the road, engrossed in conversation. The short one was waving his arms above his head and moaning 'Ooh Ray,' or something like it, and the other one, the lanky ginger kid, was hitting him and telling him to shut up. Baz smiled to himself and thought of his first holiday with his mates. He went to the Costa Brava in Spain on a mega-cheap package tour when he was seventeen with three blokes he worked with at a Kwik-Fit outfit in Enfield, his first proper job. He spent the first week desperately trying to get a shag, and then the next week desperately trying to get rid of the hound he'd eventually got off with and now wouldn't leave him alone. And he'd never been more pissed than he had during those two weeks. Great times.

Great times that were fifteen years ago. He caught sight of his reflection in the car window and suddenly felt very old, very fat, and very sad. You couldn't turn the clock back – wouldn't want to – but those times, like the suds off the car now melting into the gutter and disappearing down the storm drain, were gone for ever. And these lads, these two gawky, awkward spoddy kids had it all in front of them. Lucky bastards.

As they neared, the ginger one caught sight of the car and bashed his mate in the arm. 'Oi, Perry, look,' he said, pointing at the motor. 'Eye Ball Paul! Laaaaarge!'

'Cool!' said the short one. They ambled up to the car and waved at Baz, who smiled back. He had a horrible feeling that if they hung around, Paul was going to find some use for them, which was always a bad idea.

'Hello, lads,' said Baz, drying his hands on the towel over his shoulder. 'What you doin' 'ere?'

'Is this where Eye Ball Paul lives?' asked the ginger one, ignoring Baz's question. Baz nodded up in the direction of the balcony above them.

'That's right. He's got an apartment up there. Lives here during the summer, then he's back home for the winter. You fans, then?'

'We're DJs,' said the shorter, dumpier one, with a rather dumb grin on his face. Baz smiled. Of course they were DJs. Everyone was a DJ these days. His milkman was a DJ, his bookie was a DJ. Hell, even his granny was a DJ. 'Oi, Kev,' said the one Eye Ball christened 'Sad Act', suddenly, like he'd just remembered he'd left the iron on and the bath running. 'You got our tape on you?'

Ginger Pubes (no, his name's Kev, thought Baz to himself. Don't do Eye Ball's piss-taking for him) rummaged around in his pockets and pulled out a cassette, his face lighting up. 'Yeah, look Perry. Maybe Eye Ball Paul will listen to it, you know, in case he likes it...' said Kev, trying to act as if this was something that had just come to him at that moment.

Baz was about to give the lads the bum's rush, for their own sake, when he heard a noise above him. He looked up to the balcony and there was the man himself, Eye Ball Paul, DJ Superstar (looking pretty shitty it had to be said — an all night sesh did that to you), leaning on the balustrade and grinning like a weasel at the lads below.

'Well, look who it is,' he said, in a tone that sent shivers down Baz's spine. 'Ginger Pubes and Sad Act!' The boys, clearly star-struck and too wet behind the ears to hear the contempt in Eye Ball Paul's voice, laughed absurdly and gave him a big thumbs-up.

'Alright, Eye Ball Paul,' said Kev.

'Hur Hur, Eye Ball Paul,' said the one called Perry.

The DJ caught Baz's eye and imperceptibly motioned to him to send the boys up. Baz — who was now feeling very sorry for the two of them indeed — nodded and turned to the teenagers.

'You better follow me.' The boys leapt in the air and gave each other a high five. Baz wasn't too sure they had anything to be happy about. Still, not his business really. When it came to Eye Ball Paul and his little schemes it was best just to let things follow their natural course. Along with his other faults, the bloke had a tendency to sack people if they upset him. And right now, Baz didn't want to be sacked.

He led the boys up a narrow staircase and up to the door of the apartment. He pushed it open and led them in. Behind him, the lads gasped, and Baz understood why. Eye Ball Paul's pad was a shrine to poor taste blokedom, the ultimate naff bachelor flat. Lit around the edges of the ceiling with neon strip lights, it was decked out in black leather sofas, chrome fixtures and the odd glass-topped table. There was no natural light in the room – all the shades were drawn – and the whole effect was to make the apartment look like a shabby provincial dance club circa 1990. Paul's two club tarts – 'Muff' and 'Wankette' (ha bloody ha) – lay draped over one of the chairs together, whilst Paul stood against the far wall of the room, holding court like some ancient king. The boys stood nervously in front of him, the lanky one clutching his tape like it was the most important thing in the world. Baz suspected it may well have been.

'Erm...we brought a mix we done...' said Kev (it sounded suspiciously like the first line of a prepared speech). But before he could get any further, Eye Ball Paul lifted up a bottle of vodka from the table, unscrewed the lid, tipped his head back and then proceeded to put the rim of the bottle over his open eye, like it was an oversized bottle of Optrex. He immediately yelped and grimaced, obviously in severe discomfort.

'Aaaagh...TWAT!' he shouted, rubbing his eye, now a livid red, furiously. He turned and looked at the lads who – if they'd dropped their jaws any further – could probably have swallowed the sofa. 'Gets in your bloodstream quicker,' he said, as if pouring 40 per cent proof vodka onto your eyeball was the most natural thing in the world. This was the 'trick' which had earned him the nickname Eye Ball Paul. What a friggin' idiot, thought Baz to himself. The lads, of course, were incredibly impressed. 'Now...what were you saying?' asked Eye Ball, one side of his face now looking unpleasantly inflamed and angry.

'Er...it's just a mix we done,' stammered Kev, 'I mean you probably won't...'

'Yeah yeah yeah,' interrupted Paul with a dismissive wave of his hand. 'I thought I might give my bathroom a bit of a paint. Fancy givin' us a hand?'

The boys looked at each as if they couldn't believe their luck. Paint Eye Ball Paul's bathroom! This was way too cool. Baz looked at them and his heart sank. Here we go, he thought. Another couple of innocents fucked over by his majesty the DJ. And sure enough, they jumped at the chance.

'We'd love to!' said Kevin.

'Yeah, sorted!' added his mate.

Eye Ball Paul nodded. 'Brushes are in the cupboard in the kitchen. Give us a shout when you're finished.'

'Great. Thanks very much!' The boys shuffled off to start the job, but before they made it to the kitchen door, Eye Ball Paul called them and they turned back.

'Oh, and lads,' he said, reaching over and starting to fondle one of Muff's breasts with one hand whilst wafting his crotch with the other. 'You'll see I had a really *bangin'* shit in the bog. It won't flush, know what I mean? You'd better push it down.'

'No problem, Eye Ball,' said Kev. 'Thanks very much!' Kevin and Perry bowed and walked backwards into the kitchen, bobbing up and down like a couple of string puppets.

Eye Ball Paul snorted derisively, picked up the vodka bottle and sluiced his other eye. 'TWAT!' he shouted, slamming the bottle back down on the table.

*Yeah, you are,* thought Baz. *You most certainly are.*

It was late afternoon by the time the boys finished. They wandered along the seafront, completely shagged out, and their best kit all covered in sploshes of paint and brush marks. Eye Ball's bathroom had been a bit trickier to paint than they thought. Even so – they'd helped out the world's greatest living Dj! What a result! What a privilege!

'Eye Ball Paul is so *nice* letting us do all that work for him,' said Kevin, who hoped he'd be nice enough to let other DJs decorate his bathroom when he got famous.

'Yeah,' agreed Perry, with a little less enthusiasm. He sniffed his arm and recoiled. He'd washed it twenty times already and still the smell wouldn't go. 'Shame he didn't have a bog brush.'

'And so kind of him to give us these,' said Kevin, holding up the hard-boiled egg Eye Ball Paul had given him as a reward.

'Yeah,' said Perry, who couldn't decide which smelled worse – his arm or the egg.

'Shame his tape machine was bust,' said Kevin.

Perry nodded. 'Yeah, but he said he'd listen to it tomorrow, when we go round to help him wash his pants.'

'He is *such* a rinsin' geezer,' said Kevin, who'd spent too long listening to Big Baz on the phone. Geezer was Big Baz's favourite word. He used it lots. Twat, on the other hand, was Eye Ball Paul's favourite word. Along with 'little wanker', 'git', 'idiot', 'knob-head' and 'spacko'. He was such a cool bloke.

They walked past an elderly couple out with their dog and Perry gave them a big thumbs-up for no reason other than he felt like it. The old lady wrinkled her nose but Perry didn't much care. He'd pushed Eye Ball Paul's big sticky shit round the U-bend. How many DJs could say they'd done that, heh? That's what you did for your mates. That's what mates were for.

He was in Ibiza. He was certain to get a shag. And he'd had his fingers round the turd of the world's greatest living DJ.

It didn't get much better than this.

# chapter ten

When they got back to the apartment, Kevin's mum and dad had thankfully gone out for the day — for which Kevin was deeply grateful. He didn't think he could face them after this morning's episode. He still couldn't bring himself to admit they'd been shagging. Bouncing on the bed trying to swat a fly, maybe. Using tweezers to pull splinters out of each other's feet, possibly. Shagging, absolutely not. Never.

After a quick change of clothes — a chance for Perry to spray his arm with some Lynx deodorant Kevin brought with him — they bounced straight back out of the apartment and headed towards the beach. Not any old beach of course, but *their* beach. The beach none of the old people knew about. The beach Kev's mum and dad would never dream of going to. Kev bundled his new mini-disc player into his jacket pocket so they could listen to it with the double speaker jack Perry had picked up from the electrical store at the airport. It was a bangin' system, and on full volume it was so loud it nearly made your ears bleed.

A half hour later and the lads were on the beach. It was still hot and, not surprisingly, the sight of so many bare breasts had the identical effect as their last visit: true to form, their stiffies sprang into action and resolutely refused to disappear.

'I think I feel like sitting down,' said Perry, after ten minutes' awkward crouching. Kevin was feeling a bit strained as well, so they hobbled over to a table at the beach bar and sat themselves on a couple of stools. Any chance of stripping down to their beachwear was near nil. Not that either of them had any intention of getting out of their monsta cool puffa jackets and Stussy sweatshirts. They were just too trendy to wear anything else, and if they wanted to get the attention of any lovely ladies (who knows, maybe *their* lovely ladies) then they figured they needed to look their best.

The waiter came up and asked them if they wanted a drink, but Kevin shook his head. He'd left his money back at the apartment and the only thing he had in his pocket was the boiled egg Eye Ball Paul had given him, and he was fairly sure that wasn't legal tender in Ibiza. Anyway, he didn't want to get rid of the egg. The world's greatest living DJ had given it to him and it was without question the best holiday souvenir he'd ever had. The waiter didn't seem very happy that they weren't buying anything and shooed them away from the table – leaving them stranded and stiffied in the middle of the beach.

Then Perry came up with a de-stiffy solution, 'Hey, Kev, why don't we go for a swim? It worked last time.'

'Brilliant,' replied Kev. They lurched to the sea's edge and began wading in, jackets and all. The sound of the waves on the beach drowned out the sniggering from a few of those sunbathing near the water's edge, who couldn't believe these two kids were going into the sea fully dressed. Once they were out up to their waists, the lads turned back to the beach so they could check out the talent. Kev reached into his pocket and pulled out the two sets of headphones, one of which he handed over to Perry. They put them on and Kevin pressed the play button on his mini-disc player. Immediately their heads exploded with the thumpin' sounds of Fatboy Slim bangin' it out at the Big Beat Boutique. In perfect unison the boys nodded and tapped their water-sodden Nikes in time to the music.

Perry glanced up to the far end of the beach, and after shielding his eyes from the sun to make sure he'd got it right, elbowed Kevin in the ribs.

'WHAT IS IT?' shouted Kevin, the music filling his brain and making his teeth rattle.

'OUR LOVELY LADIES!'

'WHAT?'

'*OUR LOVELY LADIES!!*' bellowed Perry. The babbling quiet of the beach dissipated into pure silence as every couple, every girl, every bloke, every group of lads, every waiter, every beach bum, every child and every sunbather sat up to see who was shouting.

'OH YEAH!' replied Kevin. 'I TELL YOU WHAT, PERRY. WE'LL WALK PAST THEM AND PRETEND WE HAVEN'T SEEN THEM, AND THEY'LL BE SAD...'

The beach, as one, started giggling.

'...AND THEN WE'LL TURN AND GO "OH, HELLO LADIES" AND THEY'LL BE OVERJOYED!' By now there wasn't a single soul not intrigued in Kevin and Perry's next move, with the singular and rather lucky exception of Candice and Gemma, who had their own Walkmans on and were completely unaware of the little drama playing itself out in front of this huge audience of amused holidaymakers.

'I LOVE MY BLUBBERY BABE SO MUCH, KEV. SHE'S GOT LOVELY BOUNCY BOOBIES – LOOK!' Perry pointed to the other end of the beach, and like a troupe of washed-up synchronized swimmers, the beach population turned their heads in one choreographed smooth motion and looked towards where Candice and Gemma were sitting. As one, they turned back towards the boys. This was turning out to be great value for money.

The lads started wading towards the girls, but they hadn't gone four steps when Kevin felt a tug on Perry's headphone cable. He turned round to see Perry standing stock still with a very strange look on his face. 'WHAT YOU STOPPED FOR?' he yelled.

'I'M HAVIN A PISS!' shouted Perry.

'URGGHH!' went Kevin.

'Urgghh!' went the entire beach.

'YOU GOT TO HAVE A PISS IN THE SEA,' added Perry 'IT'S THE LAW.' Several of the beach audience made a mental note not to go swimming anywhere near these two if they ever saw them again. Perry, relieving himself, suddenly had a very interesting thought – I bet Gemma pisses in the sea. He thought about it for a minute. Gemma pissing in the sea. In her swimming costume. All warm and…and…and…

Then something quite untoward happened. Afterwards, looking back and trying to work out what went wrong, Perry figured it might have been because he was having a piss and getting a stiffy at the same time, made worse by the fact that he'd been a bit constipated since they got there. Whatever the reason, there was a tremendous explosion in Perry's pants, a fountain of bubbles erupted from the back of his trousers and then something long, brown and lumpy surfaced from behind him like some malignant corn-encrusted shark.

A *floater!*

'URGGHH. It's a floater!' shrieked Kevin.

'Urgghh!' went the entire beach.

Kevin stumbled backwards, but somehow the turd was caught in his slipstream. Every move he made, the poo seemed intent on pursuing him. He ducked to the left, the poo ducked to the left. He swerved to the right, the poo swerved the right. He tried to wade away as fast as he could, the poo darted ever closer.

Little did the boys know that Candice and Gemma had ventured into the sea for a quick swim. They didn't stay there very long. Looking up to see what all the commotion was about, they saw the two boys bearing down on them at great speed with what looked like a big floating turd chasing them. Realizing it *was* a big floating turd, the girls froze in abject dismay as the boys, and the turd, headed right towards them. The girls didn't have time to say anything. Two bronzed, body-sculpted beach Adonises leapt into the water like a couple of Baywatch extras and dragged the girls out of the path of the speeding poo bullet, saving them from an almost certain collision.

Kevin, meanwhile, had tripped over in his tracks. His waterlogged Nikes just weren't up to the job of sprinting through the sandy shallows of the Mediterranean, and as he stumbled backwards away from the turd, they snagged each other and brought Kevin splashing abruptly down onto his bum, his open, horrified mouth at water's level.

The turd, with an evil momentum of its own, headed straight for his gaping gob. The beach audience, turned away in a cowardly act of mass squeamishness. The boy was going to eat it, and they knew it. But then, just as the knobbly corn-cob was about to plunge into Kevin's mouth, a freak wave from a jet-skier momentarily knocked it off track and it swerved around his head, surfed the wave top and crashed to the beach. Crisis over.

'Do you think Gemma saw my poo?' lamented Perry, deeply embarrassed and humiliated by the whole floater experience. They were sitting at the harbour's edge, knocking back a couple of Cokes and trying to get their clothes dry. After getting over the initial shock of nearly gobbling Perry's bum-log, Kevin's thoughts had immediately turned to his disc-man, which he feared might have shorted-out in the water. But it seemed to be working fine, much to Kevin's relief, and as they sat watching the world go by, headphones now discarded, an idea popped into Perry's head. 'I wouldn't mind seeing Gemma's poo...' he mused, more to himself than to Kevin, who turned and gave Perry the sort of withering scornful look he usually reserved for his parents.

'Candice and Gemma do not poo...' he replied. By now Kevin hadn't so much as put the girls on a pedestal as on a hand-carved, alabaster Nelson's column with fluffy pink trim and twinkling fairy lights.

Perry nodded. 'What, like Baby Spice?'

'Now we're gonna have to think of something to really impress the girls,' pondered Kev. Just then two boys about their age puttered past on mopeds, with two pretty girls riding pillion and hugging them very tightly indeed. Kev looked at Perry. Perry looked at Kev. They both looked at the mopeds. Result!

It wasn't a bad crash. Not life-threatening, or maiming or anything. But it had hurt like mad, and Kev was still limping from where the moped had landed on his leg. Perry looked a bit dazed – there was a cut on his forehead and his arm was quite nastily grazed – but on balance, they'd come off quite lightly.

It had gone alright up 'til then. They'd gone back to the apartment for some cash, found a moped stall near the beach and hired themselves a couple of little runarounds. Neither of them had ever been on a moped before, but the bloke who rented them out didn't seem to care. In fact, he didn't seem to care about much really, except looking over his shoulder nervously as he made the deal. He disappeared for a while when a policeman walked along the seafront, and they both got the feeling he might have been just a tiny, weeny, little bit, dodgy, but all in all the boys were quite pleased. Sure, so the bikes' brakes weren't too impressive. And the tyres were a bit flat. And on Kevin's moped the handlebars hadn't quite lined up with the front wheel, whilst Perry's made this unpredictable lurch to the left whenever you changed gear. But once they were out on the road, none of this seemed to matter.

So they'd headed back towards their favourite beach looking for their girlfriends. Or soon-to-be girlfriends. Or not girlfriends. Neither of them was very certain. Either way, they hadn't been out for more than ten minutes when they saw their two love goddesses walking along the other side of the road, obviously having decided to abandon the beach and head for home.

'Afternoon ladies!' Kevin had shouted, waving as he drove unsteadily past.

Then, something of a tragedy had occurred – a lamp-post had leapt off the pavement and landed right in front of Kevin, who'd swerved and found himself next to a fruit stall and underneath the moped. Then the road had buckled violently, throwing Perry off his moped and on top of Kevin. In a few seconds the bikes went from modes of transport to articles of clothing.

'Lovely afternoon, ladies!' Perry had ventured from among the debris, in the unshakeable belief that all was not yet lost.

With haughty stares, the girls had walked on by.

It took several minutes to get the bikes untangled and the boys on their feet, by which time the girls had long since gone. 'They was impressed, weren't they

Kevin?' said Perry, limping and pushing his moped.

'Definitely,' said Kevin, checking his mouth for any broken teeth. 'Did you see the way Candice almost looked at me. She was gagging for it!'

Perry nodded enthusiastically. 'So was Gemma too. Probably. Maybe. Definitely. Gaggin' for it! Gaggin' for it large!'

The boys hitched their way back to the apartment, deeply unsure as to whether they'd had a blindingly brilliant day, or a fearsomely fucked-up day. Kevin – after a rare moment of intelligent thought – concluded that maybe there wasn't much difference.

Even so, they had to get off with the girls soon. They were desperate. And desperate men do desperate things. Everyone knew that. Even girls.

# chapter eleven

Gemma and Candice sat at the bar working out what they were going to do. They'd managed to shake Candice's mum off their tail – she'd turned into a right old nag since they got here, first moaning about the heat, then the volume of the music at night, then her sunburn, and then what time the girls were expected to be in after going clubbing. Late, Candice had said. Or maybe even really, really early. We don't know. Then her mum had gone into one about how they were only fifteen, and how they shouldn't stay out all night and how they ought to be careful and blah blah blah. Luckily for the girls, Candice's mum had to take an apartment three floors down from them because the hotel had been overbooked, which meant they were pretty much on their own. So Candice had told her mum she hated her and slammed the door, which Gemma thought was a bit unfair because she sort of liked Candice's mum, even though Candice hated her. The thing was, they'd come on holiday as a threesome, so Gemma figured maybe Candice's mum was a bit jealous that they were going out without her, but then she realized that Candice's mum was a grown-up, and grown-ups didn't get jealous like that. She didn't think so anyway.

Now that the parent situation had been sorted, the plan for the night was dead simple. They wanted to get into Amnesia. Unfortunately – as the bouncer had quite rightly pointed out – both of them were a bit on the monster side. This news wasn't as devastating as it might seem, since they both knew in their heart of hearts that beneath the zitty, sunburnt, greasy and slightly sulky-looking exteriors lay a couple of totty-tastic, horno-mongous club babes waiting to get out. Two shag-a-delic sex kittens just waiting to offer the flowers of their virginity to the right pair of lads.

The plan hinged on two vital ingredients. The first was spending a few hours having a makeover after a trip to Boots. Boots' beauty products never let anyone down. They were a girl's best friend (well, second best friend, after her first best friend – i.e. her best friend). In all probability, there had never been a greater need than now for a heavy-duty, industrial-scale Boots makeover, with all the trimmings.

The second vital ingredient was not so easy to get hold of; the two boys who were mates with Eye Ball Paul. Last night they'd watched the boys go into the club through the VIP entrance, and everyone knew that people who enter a club through the VIP entrance can do whatever they like – including getting a couple of monsters in if they wanted.

Candice took a swig of her drink as they chewed over the possibilities. 'Yeah, cos they gotta get us into the club tonight, innit.'

'It is,' replied Gemma, 'so we gotta be friendly.'

'Yeah, if we ask them in a friendly fashion,' pondered Candice.

'Yeah, we can ask them nicely and politely...' Just as she was half way through telling Candice how polite they ought to be to the boys, Gemma saw the two of them hovering over in the corner of the bar, scanning the faces of the customers. 'Oi...Candice,' she hissed, elbowing her friend in the ribs. 'It's *them!*' The two girls swiftly swung themselves round so they had their backs to the bar in the classic 'girls ignoring blokes' posture. They stayed as still as possible and stopped talking.

Kevin, who had a feeling their girlfriends might have come here, to the very beach bar where they first started going out, shoved Perry forward. 'There are our girlfriends, Pel,' he whispered. 'I think they're waiting for us.' The lads strolled up with a peculiar stiffened gait that made them look as if they had their legs in callipers and wet underwear under their trousers. 'Ladies,' said Kevin, once they'd got to the bar. In his head, he sounded suave, sophisticated, mature, erudite and exotic. Outside his head, he sounded like a bit of a tit. Luckily the girls ignored this.

Perry glanced over at Kevin, unsure as to what to do next. He coughed awkwardly. 'Ladies,' he said. No sooner had the word left his mouth than Candice swung round on her bar stool and snarled at him.

'Cos you goin' to Amnesia tonight, innit?' she barked.

'Yeah, cos you can get us in issit!' sneered Gemma, who had also swivelled round to face the lads. This was far too much information for the lads to take in at once and their brains were in serious danger of a complete system overload. This was the first time the girls had actually engaged in any sort of conversation. Actually, it was near enough the first time they'd even acknowledged their presence. And now they were talking to them and asking if they could get them into Amnesia. It was all too much really. Perry squeaked.

'Are you deaf or summink?' screeched Gemma, jolting Kevin out of his daze.

'Erm...yes, it certainly would be the greatest of pleasures to escort you into Amnesia, ladies,' he said. This was better than either of them had ever anticipated. Not only were the girls going out with them, but here was their chance to really make an impression using their cool connections in the club world. 'As it happens,' continued Kevin, 'we are best mates with Eye Ball Paul...'

'WE KNOW!' shouted the girls together, rolling their eyes like they were dealing with rather slow five-year-olds who couldn't work out how to use a spoon. With that, they jumped off their stools and stomped away. Kevin looked at Perry and they both broke into a huge grin. Just to let everyone in the bar know how pleased they were, they jumped into the air to perform a high five that looked so ridiculous the waiter burst out laughing and nearly dropped the tray he was wiping. Gemma and Candice started walking out of the bar and pausing to look back at the lads, shouted, 'Come on then!'

The walk to the girls' apartment took them in the opposite direction from where Kevin and Perry were staying and for the entire duration the girls stomped three paces ahead of the boys in silence. Not a word was said. This was really because no one could think of anything to say. Despite happily conversing with members of the opposite sex for the last thirteen years or so, since hitting puberty both the boys and the girls seemed to have lost the ability to string even the simplest of sentences together when talking to someone who might possibly, remotely, be in line for getting off with. But since both the girls and the boys felt equally uncomfortable about saying anything, the prolonged silence seemed perfectly natural.

After twenty minutes or so, they pulled up outside one of the many high-rise apartment blocks that littered the resort. As they neared the front door the girls turned to the boys. 'Wait here!' they barked, and without so much as a backward glance, they disappeared into the lobby and were eaten up by the lift doors.

The boys grinned at each other. 'Sorted!' they said in unison and, with the waiter's snide laughter having long faded to a distant echo, did another high five.

It was the only movement they'd make for a while.

*Mission: Makeover. Stage One: Zits.*

Zits could be broken down into five main categories, and the girls knew – with tragically rounded experience – exactly how each one should be managed, and in what order. First, the whiteheads. A quick scrape with the nail and they were gone. The trouble with whiteheads was that they could resurface any minute, sometimes in seconds, so if you were going to get all sweaty at a nightclub you had to watch out for each other and carry out constant whitehead patrols when in the Ladies.

Then the classic pimple. These were two-a-penny, and the girls had plenty of these. Standard procedure was to check to see whether they were ripe for harvesting – a quick, low-level squeeze from a wide base. Too much pain = not ready. But when they did go – yeuch! A quick splat (sometimes quite impressive in both distance and quantity of gunk) and then one last deep penetrating squeeze to get that hard lumpy white bit out of the middle. After doing several of these, the mirror started looking like a seagull on a diet of avocados and snails had shat on it from a great height.

The third category was the pimple mountain range – a collection of classic pimples so arranged that they were actually zits, atop zits, atop zits. These took careful route planning. The girls had to decide very carefully which ones were to be done first. Get it wrong and they could get a bleeder (and no one wants that on a night out). So, starting in the foothills they carefully squeezed each of the outlying zits until they closed in on the main peaks of the mountain range. Preparation was essential for this part of the operation, and both girls managed to reduce their Alpine faces down to something more resembling the flats of Lincolnshire, which was quite an achievement.

Both of the girls had a splendid example of a Vesuvius – a zit that had so much gunk and yuck in it that it erupted in a high-velocity explosion of green and white that never seemed to end. Gemma had one on her forehead that actually missed the mirror and splattered the door, whilst the Mount St Helens on the side of Candice's nose went with such a bang she thought she'd made herself another nostril. Both cleaned up quite nicely, so no panic there.

The last category of zit was the golf ball, which thankfully neither of the girls had. These were the really deep zits without a head on them, and they both knew from bitter experience that the temptation was to squeeze them, in increasingly harder and more painful bouts, until all you had was a huge purple lump on your chin the size of a satsuma. No, best left alone was the golf ball, no matter how much it screamed, 'Squeeze me, baby, squeeze me!'

The zits took a good hour to get sorted, but by the time the girls had finished, their faces looked less like pizzas and more like polka-dot ties – which was a definite improvement.

*Mission: Makeover. Stage Two: Body Hair.*

Both of the girls had discovered an unpleasant fact of adult life over the last couple of years. Hair. Hair everywhere. Hair poking out of their bikini bottoms.

Hair growing on their face. Hair growing out of their nose. They'd both thought, as little girls, that only men were hairy. No such bloody luck. The only reason women aren't hairy — they soon realized — is because they go through this tortuous ordeal every few weeks.

First: bikini line. No one likes looking as if they've got an army of spiders trying to escape from their gusset, and the only solution — of course — is wax. Both girls had brought more wax with them than you'd find in Madam Tussauds' chamber of horrors, and judging by the painful expression on the girls' faces as they yanked huge furry strips of the stuff from between their thighs, that was exactly where the wax had come from. Then they did their top lips (not many boys like to kiss a girl who's got a bigger moustache than they have). Fairly straightforward, but still a bit painful. Then the nostrils. Fortunately, Candice had bought a pair of heavy-duty industrial-strength nasal clippers with her, and they took turns in sticking it up each other's nostrils while watching the sink turn a fuzzy black colour. Then legs (not too tricky) and, of course, armpits (who wants to look like a garlic muncher, heh?).

*Mission: Makeover. Stage Three: Feet.*

The girls had discovered that taking a cheese-grater to the feet was far and away the easiest way to get rid of all of those lumpy bits of skin and hard patches that make feet so ugly. After whittling them down over the sink for a while, they had beautiful looking pegs and a basin that was filled with what looked like Parmesan cheese.

*Mission: Makeover. Stage Four: Head Hair.*

Wash. Condition. Blow-dry. Hate the way it's dried. Wet it again. Blow-dry it again. Hate the way it looks a second time. Slap in a handful of gel. Hate the way it looks. Wash out gel. Blow-dry. Hate the way it looks.

Put wax in it. Hate how sticky it feels. Wash out the wax. Condition it again. Leave it to dry. Curl it. Hate it. Wet it. Put it up. Hate it. Put it back down again. Leave it. Done.

*Mission: Makeover. Stage Five: Nails.*

Candice had bought a set of high-tensile, rolled, steel-reinforced, tungsten carbide, diamond-tipped clippers to get the nails on her feet sorted. And boy, did they need them. Veins the size of cattle ropes stood out on the girls' arms as they crunched the clippers on twisted, gnarled toenails which then flew off in screaming chips, ricocheting off flat surfaces and embedding themselves in the soft plaster of the wall. One bit whizzed past Candice's face so fast it left a scratch on her chin and shattered the mirror behind her with a resounding crash. Then they had to paint their toenails using highly toxic nail polish which smelled like dangerous waste products from a Russian chemical plant.

*Mission: Makeover. Stage Six: Make-up.*

It took Michelangelo most of his life to do the Sistine Chapel, which by all accounts really irritated the Pope who'd commissioned him in the first place and then had to wait thirty years for the bloke to get the job finished. What an idiot. If he'd asked a teenage girl to do it, he'd have got the entire ceiling done in a couple of hours. The works of art created on Gemma and Candice's faces were no less miraculous. (Michelangelo never had to deal with still-oozing zits, greasy pores, tufty bits of hair and razor rash.)

*Mission: Makeover. Stage Seven: Getting Dressed.*

This was the tricky one. Both girls had managed to squeeze – into two medium-sized suitcases – the entire female clothing line from Etam, Topshop, Dorothy Perkins and River Island. Like some magician's trunk, their suitcases simply filled up with more and more

clothes as more and more were taken out – a phenom-
enon which occurs with every single girl's suitcase the
world over and is the one quantum anomaly that has
prevented Stephen Hawkins from creating a unified
theory of physics. After trying on every single item at
least twice, and some as many as nine times, they eventually plumped for a couple of slinky nylon numbers
with high hemlines and plunging cleavages.

Sorted.

They stood in front of the mirror, transformed – in
a very literal sense – from spectacularly unattractive
monsters to highly desirable scrummy love ladies.

'Ready, issit?' asked Candice, playing with her hair.

'It is...' said Gemma, giving her nipples a playful
twang so they stood out just a little bit more through
the dress. 'It is.'

# chapter twelve

Down in the street, now dark and starting to fill with the usual bustle and fizz of an Ibizan Saturday night, Kevin looked at his watch.

'How long have they been?' asked Perry.

'Only about four hours,' said Kevin.

'Oh, not long then,' said Perry, who – with the potential for a snog in the near future – could well have waited days. For the three-hundred-and-twenty-ninth time that evening, they heard the bell to the lift doors in the lobby 'ting' and they turned to see who was coming out. The steel doors slid open and there – in a haze of horniness that hung around them like the scent of an expensive French perfume – stood Candice and Gemma. There was a dull thud as Kevin and Perry's jaws hit the pavement. The girls were drop-dead, traffic-stopping, plane-crashing, weather-changingly gorgeous.

The girls walked out of the doors and shot the lads a Posh Spice look as the boys tried to roll up their tongues and stuff them back into their mouths.

'Well, come on then!' they barked.

'Beautiful people, yes... Monsters, NO!' The weaselly bouncer walked up and down the line of clubbers picking out girls like a Gestapo officer. In his pocket he had a stack of vanity mirrors ready to do his 'breaking my mirror means you're a pig' routine that worked so well in making the girls cry. It was the best bit of the job. Watching them slope off with their tails between their (usually fat) legs. He loved it. Ugly birds made him happy, cos ugly birds helped him forget what a git he was. And like his old man used to say, if you can't be big, and you can't be clever, and you can't be good looking and you can't be successful — be a bully. Well, actually his old man hadn't said it at all, but if he had, it would have been a fackin' brilliant thing to say.

No one knew he wasn't a real bouncer of course — except the *real* bouncers, and they didn't seem to mind him weeding out the trogs before they got to the main entrance. He considered himself a charity worker — selflessly sacrificing himself night after night so all the decent fellas in the world didn't have to go to clubs and spend all night looking at a bunch of dogs' arses. Not that any of them thanked him for it. But then it wasn't thanks he was after. He just wanted to make ugly women cry. Ugly women just like his ex-girlfriend…

…the SLAG…

…who didn't deserve to go to any club, ever. Or look at another bloke. Especially big ones who worked in the meat department at Sainsbury's…

…the BASTARD…

He was about to smash another mirror — thinking once more of the big bloke from the meat counter at Sainsbury's who'd run off with his Sharon — when the crowd starting making a fuss at something behind him. He looked over his shoulder and there, strolling up towards the entrance was the DJ, Eye Ball Paul. 'Alright Paul, owzit 'angin?' said the real bouncer as the star walked to the door.

'Largin' it,' muttered the DJ under his breath. He marched through the entrance followed by an entourage made up of his driver, the two club tarts he had with him the night before, two spoddy little kids and, right at the back, a couple of tasty-looking birds who looked strangely familiar. The weaselly one shrugged, turned back to the girl he was talking to and picked up where he left off.

'Anyway... beautiful people, yes, monsters, NO. You...are a MONSTER!' Smash! went the mirror, and the girl started to cry. The bouncer grinned and moved down the line. Ugly birds. Brilliant!

While he was picking out his next trog, four lads in the queue huddled in a circle and examined the contents of a small zip-top plastic bag that one of them had pulled from his pocket.

'What are they exactly?' asked one, checking over his shoulder to make sure none of the bouncers were watching.

'Dunno,' said his mate blithely. He'd just bought the pills from some dealer on the corner, and although he didn't have a clue what was in them, (there was a cruddy picture of a dog on each, not that it meant anything – they could be full of flea powder) he was fairly certain they couldn't do him any harm. He reached into the bag and took out the four pills, distributing them around his friends. 'Lift-off in an hour, gentlemen. Fasten your seatbelts!' he said, swigging back his E with a bottle of water and then handing it to his friends. They laughed, took their drugs and then tried to get themselves looking sensible for the bouncers. Sorted at Amnesia! Nothing could go wrong.

It was Big Baz that got them in really. Kevin and Perry had taken the girls round to Eye Ball Paul's pad in the hope that the DJ would get them into the club, but when they arrived Eye Ball Paul was already stepping into the limo and didn't notice them screaming, shouting and waving their arms over their heads as he got in. Baz – luckily – did, once he'd closed the door on Paul, and beckoned the lads over.

'The guvnor's a bit…distracted tonight, boys,' he said, keeping his voice low so the two girls couldn't hear. 'Probably best if he goes in with his lady friends on his own tonight.' The boys' faces fell into a crumpled heap around their chins and Baz could see the disappointment dripping off them like sweat. He sighed and looked over the road to the taxi rank. He didn't want to get these boys caught up with Eye Ball Paul any more than he had to, but they'd obviously come out hoping to impress the two girls and he'd probably ruin their night – if not entire holiday – if he sent them home empty-handed and humiliated in front of the little lasses. Oh bugger it, he thought, what the hell. He pointed to the row of little yellow Fiats. 'What you wanna do is grab yourselves a cab and head for the club,' he said. 'When we get there, I'll have to park out back and walk round with His Majesty, so hang around near the front door 'til we turn up. Then just tag behind me when I go in and you'll have no problems.' He looked up to make sure the girls were listening, and then said in a loud voice 'Eye Ball Paul wants you to be his guests at the club tonight lads, so follow me and you'll get the usual VIP treatment.' He turned back to the boys and winked. 'See you later, lads…'

They'd done as he'd said, and sure enough, twenty minutes later, they'd strolled through the front doors of Amnesia with their new best mate Eye Ball Paul in front, and their girlfriends in tow behind. Their new *horny* girlfriends, who were quite clearly impressed at the way they'd simply walked past all the bouncers without saying a word, and most importantly, without spending a peseta.

Now – on the dance floor stacking boxes, doing big fish little fish and opening curtains – neither of them thought life could get any better. Their girlfriends had mysteriously disappeared the moment they got through the door, but neither of the boys thought too much of it. Girls did stuff like that – vanishing in the middle of a conversation, whispering to their friends and giggling at you, ignoring you altogether – so neither took much notice.

'Top choon!' shouted Kevin to Perry as Eye Ball Paul cranked up the pace a bit and another Ibizan anthem pounded out of the speakers.

'Choon!' yelled Perry over the thumping bass, holding his two glow sticks above his head in the shape of a letter T. This was too good. This was beyond good. All that was missing were their two lovely ladies... Just then he caught sight of them dancing underneath a balcony on the other side of the dance floor. He grabbed Kevin's arm, 'Look Kev, it's my blubbery girl-friend and your lovely lady.'

'Cool!' replied Kevin, as they headed off in the direction of the girls, stacking boxes and closing curtains as they went. It took them a while to wriggle through the heaving mass of sweaty, trancing dancers – including the line of formation-dancing, mega-naff Germans they'd seen the night before and some weirdo dressed up as a suitcase – but by the time they made it, the girls had seen them coming and had impercepti-bly made a space for them on the floor. The lads got nearer and Kevin shouted 'Ladies!' waving energeti-cally. Just as they got to within talking distance there was a repulsive splashing sound and Kevin suddenly found himself drenched in something warm, wet and lumpy. He took a cautious sniff.

Puke.

He looked up through the blanket of chunder covering his face and saw four lads – all looking decidedly green and unhealthy – leaning over the balcony. 'Sorry mate,' one of them shouted down, wiping his mouth with the back of his hand. As he did so, something fluttered out of his pocket and landed at Perry's feet. It was a small, zip-top plastic bag. Perry picked it up and was about to tell the bloke he'd dropped it when the bloke standing next to him heaved forward and also puked over the balcony, right on Perry's head.

There was an audible gasp from the dancers, the music stopped, and everyone pulled back leaving the boys standing on their own in a small circular clearing.

Silence.

Perry looked at Kevin, who had something mushy and orange sliding down his cheek, and decided the best policy would be to carry on as if nothing had happened. He turned to Gemma. 'Love the shapes you're pulling la…'. He got no further. Another splash of vomit hit him right on the head and slid down the back of his shirt. 'Sorry mate,' came a second cry from upstairs. Perry – trying not to look like he was the sort of dude who gets upset when he's puked on – looked up to give the bloke a thumbs-up when both he and Kev caught a face full of fresh vom. The crowd groaned in sympathy. Instinctively, they knew that try as they might, they couldn't make a night of it after this.

'G'night ladies…' said Kevin, trying to maintain as much dignity as possible.

'G'night ladies,' said Perry. They turned to go and the crowd divided in front of them, none of the clubbers wanting to get near the two sick-covered boys.

'G'night Germans,' said Kevin.

'G'night Part Man, Part Luggage,' said Perry to the man in a suitcase. They reached the door and as they stepped out into the cool air, heard the music start up again behind them.

Neither of them saw the two bronzed beach Adonises – the ones who'd rescued the girls from the floater – move in and start talking to Candice and Gemma once they'd left.

# chapter thirteen

The cosmic scales of justice had once again put Kevin and Perry's holiday on an even footing. To compensate for the sheer magnificence of walking into Amnesia behind the world's greatest living DJ Eye Ball Paul, and with two gorgeously beautiful top totties at their side, the gods had levelled off the karma by publicly covering them both in fresh puke. From the highest of the highs they'd plunged to the lowest of the lows. Kevin and Perry's rollercoaster ride weighed in at net zero, and their depression could not have been greater if their stiffies had fallen off.

'We were so nearly there,' lamented the freshly laundered Perry, staring at the ceiling in their bedroom. 'Maybe we shouldn't have left. Maybe the girls wouldn't have minded if we were covered in puke.'

'They would have minded,' said Kevin with a dull, flat conviction.

'I wouldn't mind if Gemma was covered in puke. I'd still shag her...' Perry tailed off, his eyes glazing over and his bedspread slowly rising into the familiar tent-pole position. Kevin looked over and shook his head. Perry was sick and Kev had had enough. He was tired. He was depressed. Most of all, he was bored. Bored with the inevitability of failure. Every time he tried to make a go of something, every time things started to go right, something went horribly, drastically wrong. It was as if someone, somewhere, had control of his life and was deliberately trying to get him to commit suicide. Whoever it was, he was a bastard. If he didn't know better, he'd have said it was his parents. Perry's voice droned on and Kevin closed his eyes. Bored. Bored of Perry. Bored of the holiday. Bored of life. Bored. Bored. Bored...

'When Eye Ball Paul plays our mix they'll love us for ever. Everything's gonna be alright, innit Kev? Kev? *Kev?*' Perry looked over and saw, in the moonlight, that Kevin's eyes were closed and he was snoring gently. 'Kev? You awake, Kev?' There was no response, and so Perry turned onto his back and resumed staring at the ceiling. The night was eerily calm. Through the open doors to the balcony Perry could hear the cry of a gull and the gentle wash and swell of the waves on the beach. And he could also hear... what? Giggling? He cautiously lifted his head off the pillow to have a better listen and sure enough, through the wall, he heard a loud and infectious giggle. Mrs Patterson's giggle. And then...creaking. A bed creaking. And more giggling. He sat up as quietly as he could and swung his legs out of the bed. Reaching onto the bedside table for his digi-cam, Perry froze as he heard Mrs Patterson moan.

'Oooh Ray...' came the low groan from next door. 'Mmm... Oh Ray...' Perry made a tiny 'wheeerp!' noise, steadied himself on the edge of Kev's bed and then padded silently out of the room, careful not to nudge any of the furniture or trip over Kevin's stuff lying all over the floor. He crept out onto the balcony, and keeping in the shade of the moonlight cast by the flowers and undergrowth coming off the roof, sneaked up to Mr and Mrs Patterson's window. Slowly raising himself to peep through the shutters and steal a quick glance, he nearly toppled over backwards.

Mr and Mrs P. were doing it. *Doing it!* Mr P. was lying on his back with his hands handcuffed (*handcuffed!!!*) to the bedstead, with Mrs P. straddling him and moving up and down at an ever-increasing speed. They were both moaning with pleasure, Mrs Patterson's 'Oh Rays' getting louder and louder. Perry emitted a barely audible squeak and had to steady himself as his legs went wobbly. He had a stiffy fit to burst. Oh God...this was the horniest thing he'd ever seen. Better than a porno mag. Better than a porno film. *Porno film!* He looked down at the digi-cam in his hand. Why had he brought it out? He didn't know. But since he had it...

He flipped up the viewfinder, turned it on, and lifted it above his head so it got an uninterrupted view of Mr and Mrs P. shagging. And then he slumped involuntarily down against the wall, his arm above his head holding the camera. Something had happened in his trousers.

Now he knew why they called it a knee trembler.

'Well, here we are,' said Kevin jauntily as the boys bounced along the street towards Eye Ball Paul's flat. Kev felt much better this morning. He'd realized over breakfast that they still had plenty of time to get off with their girlfriends, and once they'd heard the lads' mix – thanks to their new best mate Eye Ball Paul – the girls would be powerless. They'd probably shag them there and then, right in the club, in front of everyone. Kevin pulled the tape from his bag and waved it in front of Perry's face. 'He promised to listen to it today.'

'Yeah – cos he's our new best mate, in'ee Kev?' said Perry, with a daft grin on his face. Kevin shrugged. Perry was weird sometimes, and he'd had that stupid look on his face since they'd got up this morning. Kev thought maybe Perry had had a brilliant wank the night before. That might have cheered him up. It often cheered Kevin up, anyway.

They bounded up the steps to the apartment and banged on Eye Ball Paul's door. Now they were cookin'! Kevin grasped the tape even tighter. Eye Ball Paul was sure to love their mix. Why else would he want them to come over?


'Owzit goin' Sad Act?' asked Eye Ball Paul, looking down at Perry and Kevin who were on their hands and knees scrubbing the stone floor of the kitchen with thick brushes, a bucket of soapy water beside them.

'Really well, thanks Eye Ball Paul!' replied Perry, dunking the brush back into the bucket and wincing slightly at the foul odour coming up from the floor.

'So, er, you got that tape then,' Eye Ball Paul asked distractedly.

Kevin and Perry stopped scrubbing and looked up. 'Er… yeah, it's in our beach bag,' said Kevin, barely able to disguise his excitement. 'I'll go and get it.' He started to get up but Eye Ball Paul waved him back down with a curt sweep of his hand.

'No, don't worry. I'll find it. You carry on scrubbing.' He left the kitchen in a haze of cigarette smoke and bad breath.

'He's gonna listen to it, Pel!' whispered Kevin, giving his mate a big thumbs-up.

'Our tape!' squeaked Perry, unable to believe their luck. The world's greatest living DJ, and their new best mate, Eye Ball Paul, was going to listen *to their mix*es! They carried on scrubbing, even more eager to do a better job for Eye Ball Paul. Which is exactly what he wanted.

In the lounge Eye Ball Paul stepped over the two new (unconscious) club tarts he'd brought home with him last night and reached into the scuffed beach bag Perry had left by the side of the sofa. He pulled out a swanky looking digi-camera which he put down on the glass-topped, slightly powdery coffee table and then rooted around again to find the tape. He eventually found it, stuck it in his deck and pressed the play button. The opening bars to Kevin and Perry's 'Big Girl' pounded out of the speakers, and without even letting it get to the first chorus Eye Ball Paul punched the eject button and the tape slid smoothly out of the machine. 'What a bunch of wank...' he scoffed quietly, chucking the tape onto a heap of cassettes on the floor.

Looking back in the bag, his attention was drawn by the video camera, much more his thing than some stupid mix done by those sad kids. The camera was small and neat, with a nifty little fold-out screen and great looking chrome buttons. 'This is well hammerin'...' he said, flipping open the viewing screen and pressing the play button.

In the kitchen, Perry overheard the comment. 'He said our choon's well hammerin', Kev!'

'Oh wow, man!' said Kev, thrilled at Eye Ball Paul's reaction to their music. From the front room came a roar of approval and Kevin and Perry stopped scrubbing the floor so they could hear the DJ. He loved their choons! This was way cool.

'Tits up!' shouted Eye Ball Paul from next door. 'Talk about 'avin it large!' The boys were beside themselves with pride. If ever there was a good judge of happenin' choons, Eye Ball Paul was it. And he loved their stuff. You only had to listen to him to know he thought it was wicked. Havin' it large indeed!

His head appeared in the doorway and the boys looked up expectantly. 'Boys!' said Eye Ball Paul. 'I like the tape!'

'Yeah?' replied Kevin and Perry, trying to sound as casual as they could, which was fairly difficult since neither of them had ever felt less casual in their entire lives.

'Yeah,' replied the DJ. 'I thought we could play it again large. Fancy joining me and Baz?'

'Sure!' said Kevin, starting to get to his feet.

'Tut! Tut! Tut!' scolded Eye Ball Paul, waving his finger at them. '*When* you've finished the floor.'

'Yeah,' said Kevin.

'Course…' said Perry.

Eye Ball Paul grinned and gave them a thumbs-up. Way cool! The boys' hands became a blur as they scrubbed the floor like their lives depended on it.

Baz stood at the back of the room wondering what Eye Ball Paul was up to now. He'd overheard the conversation between Paul and the kids but didn't think for a minute Eye Ball Paul would actually listen to the kids' music, let alone admit to liking it. Yet he told them he thought it was 'large' and 'bangin' and 'monsta'. He was up to something, and it smelled bad.

The lads appeared in the doorway to the lounge, drying their hands on a towel and looking eagerly around the room. 'Finished, Eye Ball Paul,' said Kevin.

'That was quick,' remarked the guv'nor, fiddling with the TV control.

'No sweat,' said Perry cheerfully and rather inaccurately, since he was dripping in the stuff.

'Sit yourselves down, lads,' said Eye Ball Paul, waving at a gap between the two club babes on the leather upholstery. The girls – vacant and spacey – shifted up to make more room for the boys to sit down in front of the TV. Eye Ball Paul drew himself upright. 'Twattia, Buttasha,' he said, 'Watch this. You might learn a trick or two!'

Kevin frowned. 'Watch? You mean listen...hur, hur!'

'No,' said Eye Ball Paul, emphatically. 'I mean... *watch*.' He flicked a button on the remote control of the television and an image sprang into view. It was a bedroom, with two moving figures in it. Kevin was just leaning forward to work out what it was, when the picture suddenly became brighter, as if the camera that took it had abruptly compensated for the poor light.

'Oooh Ray...' came his mother's voice from seven speakers dotted around the room.

A low strangled gurgle came from Kevin who could not believe what he was seeing. The screen was filled with the image of his mum and dad having sex. Very energetic, saucy and intimate sex. Perry whimpered and looked desperately at Eye Ball Paul with complete disbelief.

Eye Ball Paul, seeing the expression on both their faces, burst out laughing, a cruel and hysterical high-pitched squawk usually only heard in buildings with lots of padded rooms and long-sleeved white jackets. This was too fuckin' funny. What a couple of twats! What a couple of wankers! It was too much, really, too fuckin' much...

Kevin's eyes were the size of headlamps and his jaw lay slack round his ankles. 'No...' he muttered. 'No, no, no, no, no...'

Perry, pole-axed by guilt and burning shame, glanced over at his mate and squeaked, 'Sorry, Kev.'

Kevin turned on Perry with a ferocious sneer. 'Perry, you bloody pervert!'

Kevin leapt to his feet and took two strides over to the near-frenzied Eye Ball Paul. 'Can we have our tape back please,' he demanded in a passably intimidating tone.

'Oh dear...' guffawed the DJ, clutching his sides. 'Oh dear oh dear oh dear...' He took the tape out of the machine and went to offer it to Kevin but then pulled it back as soon as Kev reached for it.

'Please Eye Ball Paul...'

'She's a randy little bitch your mum, isn't she?' goaded the lanky DJ, holding the tape above his head as Kevin lunged for it. 'Bangin' tits for an old bird.'

'NO!' screamed Kevin, making one last move for the tape and failing. His humiliation complete, he stormed out. Perry, who had also leapt to his feet by now, scurried after him, shaking all over like he'd been badly scalded.

Big Baz looked at Eye Ball Paul with a look of pure, unadulterated contempt. What a scumbag. What a dirt-sucking, shit-licking, fart-sniffing, fuckwit. Baz clenched his fist and eyed the boss with a steely stare. 'Give him his tape back,' he said menacingly.

'Fuck off Baz, you soft twat,' sneered Eye Ball Paul 'I'll give it back to him later.' And with that Eye Ball Paul put the tape into his video, and pressed record on his sampler. 'Oooh Ray...' the sound of Kevin's mother at the peak of a particularly impressive, and highly personal orgasm, filled Eye Ball's lounge.

Baz let his hand relax, took a deep breath, and walked calmly out of the room. That was it. Adios amigo, as they said in these parts. All he had to do now was pick his moment.

And there was plenty of time to do that. Oh yes, indeed.

# chapter fourteen

Kevin stumbled along the seafront in a daze, the world around him blurred by hot tears. Perry had betrayed him. His best friend, his only mate, *his soul-mate*, was a sick pervert who went round filming people's parents having sex. The revulsion he felt at seeing his parents *doing it* was gone, now replaced by a burning, swirling anger. His parents — had they seen into Kev's head right then — would have been surprised that alongside his tearful childishness also appeared one of his first ever truly mature thoughts. Kevin realized that his parents' privacy had been violated, and even though Kev thought what they were doing was disgusting, it was still *their* disgusting. No one should see it. Not Perry. Not some DJ. And certainly not Kev himself.

But worse than all this — the most painful thing — was the fact that he could never be friends with Perry again. Ever. Perry had broken the rules. And you *never* broke the rules with your best mate. You never tried to shag your mate's girlfriend. You never grassed on your mates to anyone. You never took sides against your mate in an argument. And you never, ever, ever filmed your mate's mum and dad having filthy, perverted sex with handcuffs and stuff.

124

This was no adolescent hormonal strop. Kevin was deeply, genuinely (and as he thought, possibly fatally) hurt. Life was truly dreadful.

He wanted his mum. He wanted to play footie with his dad. He wanted a hug.

'Kev! Kev! Sorry mate!' Perry scurried behind Kevin, trying to keep up with his friend's furious, stomping strides.

'You are not my mate and you are not my fellow DJ!' shouted Kevin, his voice hitching in raw, breathless sobs. He wiped away the tears on his face with his sleeve. 'Goodbye for ever!' And with that, Kevin broke into a run, oblivious to everything except the awful, aching grief that filled him from head to toe.

Perry stopped, rooted to the spot. He watched his best friend disappear down the promenade, a gangling, loping mess of puffa jacket, baggy dockers and tangled ginger hair. His best mate, who he loved cos he was the best mate anyone could want in the whole world.

His ex-best mate.

Perry put his hands in his pocket, leaned against the concrete sea wall, and started crying. For Kevin. For himself. For their friendship.

It was over.

Kevin ran forever. He ran 'til his legs simply wouldn't take him any further and his lungs refused to draw in a single breath. He staggered to a stop and stood clutching his sides, then slumped onto the steps of a small fountain that stood in the middle of a market square. His eyes were red and swollen through so much weeping and he rested his head in his hands – his temples pounding. A stray dog wandering past the fountain came and sat next to him, a similar look of rejection and despair hanging from its canine jowls. Kevin put his arm around

125

the dog and stared at the people passing by. The dog was now his only friend. He had nothing.

It was – with no exaggeration at all – the worst day of his entire life. Things couldn't be worse. He couldn't sink any lower if he got a spade and started digging.

A tinkle of laughter broke through his depression and he looked up. There were Candice and Gemma, walking across the square towards the beach with the two Adonis boys from yesterday. Walking arm in arm. Laughing. Just like boyfriends and girlfriends.

*Boyfriends?*

Kevin let out a low, wounded moan. His best mate was a sicko *and* his girlfriend had chucked him for someone else. He jumped to his feet and ran away sobbing, covering his face with his hands. It *had* got worse. Much worse.


Perry stood on the promenade looking out to sea with a dull, sick feeling in his stomach. He hadn't wanted this to happen. He was just mucking about with the camera and he hadn't really meant to film Mr and Mrs Patterson. At least he didn't think he had. Sometimes he did stuff without thinking about it – like setting fire to that rubbish bin at school and making all the alarms go off. Or when he secretly peed in the drawer of his Form Master's desk after detention one night. Stuff like that just sort of happened. And he'd got a bit worse since his mum and dad had split up. It was like he couldn't help himself sometimes.

And now...now look what he'd done. Lost his best mate. His only mate. Filmed Kev's mum and dad shagging. When he thought about it – which he hadn't done yet – it was a bit of a stinky thing to do. It was like someone taking pictures of you having a wank, and Perry was pretty sure he wouldn't like anyone to do that to him.

Question was — what would he do without Kev? Kev, who always made him laugh when he was in trouble. Kev, who lived in a house with proper parents and had nice stuff. Kev, the best bloke on the planet.

His eyes filled up with tears again and he shuffled away from the wall and down the steps to the beach, trying to work out what to do. He trudged along the sea's edge scuffing stones with his Reeboks and thinking maybe he should ring his mum tonight. He'd like to hear her voice, just to say hello, tell her he was having a good time. He wouldn't tell her what had happened. He wouldn't tell *anyone* what had happened.

He stopped next to a little boy who was building a sandcastle. Perry looked down at him and smiled wanly. He used to like making sandcastles when he was small. One summer, when his mum and dad were still together, they went to the Isle of Wight on holiday and Perry had built this enormous castle with his dad. It had turrets and a moat and little roads made out of seashells and knights made out of broken lolly sticks. It was brilliant.

But that was a long time ago. Another world. Another life.

'Need a hand?' asked Perry, when the little boy looked up.

'OK,' said the boy, so Perry fell to his knees and grabbed a handful of sand. For a while, he was seven again, on the Isle of Wight, with his mum and his dad.

That was fine.

Kevin made it back to the apartment and wearily climbed the steps to the balcony. He pulled up a chair and sat looking out to sea, wondering what he should tell his mum and dad. The thought of talking to them about...sex...especially *them* and...and sex...urrggh. It was too much. He couldn't tell them. Anyway, they'd never know. They didn't have to be told.

He heard a noise behind him and glanced round through pink, puffy eyes to see his mum looking down at him with a concerned look on her face. 'What's up, love?' she asked, sitting down next to him and taking his hand in hers.

'Kevin?' said his dad softly from behind.

'I... I... I want to go home...' he managed to get out between broken gasps, before his mum put her arms round his shoulders and he collapsed onto her chest, a big, blubbering wreck.

'Oh dear...' she said, glancing over at Ray, who looked as worried as she felt. 'Have you had a row with Perry?' she asked, knowing full well what the answer would be. After all, where there was Kevin, there was Perry. And Perry was nowhere to be seen. Kevin nodded, and his mum – for the first time in several years – gave him the comfort of a cuddle, and a kiss on his mop of unruly hair.

'Would you like a cup of tea, old man?' asked his dad, patting him on the shoulder.

'Yeth, muf, please Dad,' snuffled Kevin.

'Oh, love. Everything's going to be alright,' soothed his mum. A few moments later Dad came onto the balcony with a cup of tea, which Kevin, sitting up in his chair, gratefully took off him with a thin smile. Tea, the great restorative, soon worked its magic and Kevin's crying gradually subsided.

'I tell you what,' suggested his dad. 'Why don't we all go out for a nice meal? Would you like that, old man?'

'Oh, that would be lovely,' said his mum, smiling. 'Let's smarten up and go out. Just the three of us, heh?' Kevin nodded mutely. There was comfort in cups of tea and going out for food with just his mum and dad. It was kids' stuff, but sometimes kids' stuff was OK. Sometimes kids' stuff was perfect.

With a final pat of his spade, Perry finished the retaining wall to the bottom moat and sat back on his haunches to look at his handywork. It looked mightily cool. Four big sandcastles, linked by four moats, two walkways, several arched bridges, a big wall around the four of them, and spectacularly decorated with seashells, pebbles and – at the little boy's insistence – a Kit Kat wrapper. The little boy delicately stuck a tiny paper flag into the biggest of the castles and turned to Perry. 'You're my best friend,' he said resolutely.

Perry was about to reply when he heard someone cough behind him. He jumped up to find himself face-to-face with Gemma, who, together with Candice, stood with arms wrapped around two muscly blond boys, the ones who'd been at the beach before. That meant... that meant Gemma wasn't his girlfriend any more. He felt his bottom lip tremble but was powerless to stop it.

'Cos what happened to you last night was well bad,' said Gemma suddenly. Perry gawped, not sure what to say.

'What happened?' asked Gemma's new boyfriend.

'Got puked on,' replied Gemma, matter-of-factly.

'What a bummer,' said the boyfriend, his handsome face creasing into a frown.

'You alright?' asked Gemma to Perry, who was now on the verge of bursting into tears. Perry was definitely not alright. He'd never been more not alright.

'Is he your boyfriend?' he blurted out, pointing to the boy who had his arm round Gemma's lovely tummy.

'No, he's *my* boyfriend,' said the boy who had his arm round Candice. Perry looked from one to the other, trying to work out what the boy meant, and then, in an instant, it all made sense.

'Hur!' he guffawed clumsily. 'Bum boys!'

'No, gay lovers!' said Gemma, with a self-conscious air of political correctness about her.

'Oh yeah, sorry,' mumbled Perry, overjoyed that the lovely blubbery lady was still *his* lovely blubbery lady.

'That your sandcastle?' asked Gemma, pointing at Perry's gargantuan creation.

'Oh, um… well, I was just helping the little kiddie,' he said pointing embarrassedly at the boy, who looked a bit miffed that his new best mate called him little.

'Cos Perry's got an artistic nature,' said Gemma to no one in particular. 'Cos you've got a sensitive nature.' She looked at Perry and smiled sweetly. Perry felt an immediate and all-too familiar stirring in his trousers Gemma liked him! *Really, properly, not-make-believe, liked him*! He tried casually to cover his crotch, a move that went unnoticed by the girls but not the boys, who gave him a slightly disbelieving wide-eyed look.

'Where's Kevin, issit?' asked Candice suddenly.

'Er…dunno,' replied Perry.

'He's alright,' said Candice. Even Perry knew that 'alright' was the greatest accolade a boy could get from a girl. 'We're coming clubbin' wiv you and Kev tonight, yeah?' Perry's head reeled. This was all happening too suddenly. Candice liked Kevin. Gemma liked Perry. They were going to go clubbing tonight.

He had to find Kevin and tell him.

The girls turned and started to walk off, and as they went, Gemma looked back over her shoulder and gave Perry a long and languorous wink. 'Later,' she mouthed, and winked again.

'Later…' squeaked Perry in excitement. Wow! For a moment his limbs refused to obey any instruction coming from his brain. He just stood there, hyperventilating like a landed fish and grinning inanely. Then his body finally caught up with his head, and he scuttled off in the opposite direction to the girls, back towards the apartment.

As he went, the little boy looked after him in confusion 'Where are you going?'

'I've gotta go home. See you later.' said Perry, preoccupied by the thought of the coming evening. The little boy grinned and gave him a thumbs-up. He liked Perry. What wasn't there to like?

Perry hurried along the seafront, anxious to get back and tell Kevin the news, when there was an unexpected screech of brakes and Eye Ball Paul's limo slid to a sudden stop in the road next to him. The window wound down and the DJ poked his head out. 'Oi, Sad Act,' he said, lifting Perry's beach bag into view. 'You forgot this.'

Perry didn't know what to say. Was Eye Ball Paul mucking about or was he really going to give the bag back? He tentatively reached out to grab it, and as Eye Ball Paul made no move to snatch it away, he took it from the DJ's hand. Then Eye Ball Paul held up the digicam and Kevin and Perry's demo tape. 'And this!' he said, handing them to him through the window.

'Thanks, Eye Ball Paul,' said Perry.

'I like your mix,' said the DJ, as if he was embarrassed to admit it. 'It's cool. Think I'll use it in the set tonight at the club. Want a lift there?' Perry nodded mutely. 'You and Ginger Pubes. My pad. Tonight. Now fuck off.' The DJ slapped the side of the car and it drove off, the tinted window sliding up and hiding Eye Ball Paul's face from view.

Perry's brain was close to a complete system meltdown. The girls were going to shag them *tonight.* Eye

**Ball Paul was going to play their mixes *tonight*. It was all going off *and Kevin didn't know a thing about it*!**

Perry broke into a run. He had to find Kev.

# chapter fifteen

'So what's happened between Kevin and Perry?' whispered Mr Patterson, checking his tie in the mirror. He'd booked them in at a lovely restaurant in the centre of town. It was a bit spendy, but Kevin needed cheering up, and anyway it had been a long time since they'd all gone out together as a family without Kevin throwing a wobbly. Of course, it stood to reason he didn't want to see Kevin upset, but it was kind of nice to have him back to normal, at least for a while.

'I've no idea,' replied his wife, spraying her wrists with the new perfume she'd bought in duty-free. 'You know what boys are like, Ray. Storm in a teacup, I suspect. Anyway, not really our business is it? If we want Kevin to act like an adult I suppose we should treat him like one and not stick our noses in. Whatever it is, I hope he and Perry make it up. Might make things a bit awkward around here if they don't.'

Mr Patterson was about to reply when there was clatter on the staircase and Perry burst into the room through the front door, breathless and sweaty.

'Mr, Mrs Patterson...' he gasped, skidding to a halt. 'Where's Kev?'

'He's in the bedroom, Perry,' said Mr Patterson sombrely.

'He's quite upset,' said Mrs Patterson (who strangely didn't look very sexy now to Perry, even though she was all tarted up and everything). 'You'd better go and make up.'

'Erm...yeah,' said Perry nervously. He went to the door and hovered with his hand above the handle. What if Kev told him to piss off again? That would be bad. What if Kev never spoke to him again? It didn't bear thinking about. He knocked on the door but there was no response.

'In you go, Perry,' said Mr Patterson, giving him *the look*. Perry had never had *the look* before. Kevin got it all the time. It made Perry feel sort of good and bad at the same time.

He nervously twisted the door handle and pushed the door open until it was wide enough for him to step in, cautiously closing it behind him.

Kevin was sitting on the bed, staring out of the balcony windows. He had on one of his dad's shirts and ties, and Perry thought he looked a bit silly, although that was absolutely the last thing he would tell Kev, now or ever. 'Alright, Kev?' asked Perry timidly. Kevin ignored him and continued looking out the window. Perry scratched himself, unsure what to do or say.

'Sorry, Kev.'

There was an awkward silence while Kevin contin-ued to stare for what felt like for ever. Then he stood up and walked stiffly over to Perry, carefully avoiding looking at him, and silently extended his hand for Perry to shake.

*Perry was forgiven!*

Feeling ecstatic, but knowing the situation still demanded a certain formality, Perry extended his own hand and they shook with great seriousness.

And they shook.

And shook.

And shook.

And shook.

'Thanks, Kev,' sniffled Perry eventually, feeling himself starting to go all weepy. The emotions over-whelmed him and he flung his arms around Kev in a big bearhug. Kev, not sure what to do, did nothing. But then he too started to feel like blubbing. Perry was his mate again. Perry, the best mate a bloke could have. Perry, a bit weird, but OK. Perry – his-best-mate-fellow-DJ! Kevin burst into tears and for a few precious moments the lads hugged each other and cried openly without any embarrassment and without any shame.

Which, of course, didn't last long.

They coughed self-consciously and extracted them-selves from the hug with renewed formality. 'Erm... why you got a tie on Kev?' asked Perry, still sniffling.

'Going for a meal with my mum and dad,' replied Kev, swallowing back the snivels.

'Had a nice afternoon?'

'Not very good. How about you?'

Perry shrugged. 'I built a sandcastle.'

Kevin nodded. He understood that making a sand-castle was OK. Then he wondered if Perry knew the bad news. 'Candice and Gemma have got new boyfriends,' he sniffled. 'I saw them in the street with two blond bigger boys...' He trailed off, the thought of his girlfriend with someone else sure to get him blubbing again.

'No,' said Perry excitedly. 'They're blond bigger bum boys...oh, I mean, gay lovers.'

'What?'

'I saw them on the beach with Candice and Gemma. They're gay lovers! And they're just friends. And...and Gemma said I was sensitive and wanked at me...no, I

135

mean, winked at me. And Candice asked where were you and said you was alright.'

Kevin couldn't believe his ears. Candice *asked where he was* and then (and this was the clincher) said *he was alright.* 'Candice said I was alright?' he repeated, wanting to be sure Perry hadn't made a mistake. Saying someone was alright was a big deal. Possibly the biggest.

'Yeah, and they wanna see us at the club tonight!'

Kevin was overjoyed. And just when things couldn't get any happier, Perry held up the tape from the digi-cam. 'And I got this from Eye Ball Paul for you.' Perry took a deep breath. He'd been practising the next bit all afternoon, while he was making the sandcastle, and he'd gone over it in his head so many times now he almost thought it was the truth himself. In a few weeks time, it would be the truth, the only truth. 'Sorry Kev, I didn't do it on purpose,' he started. 'What happened was, I couldn't sleep so I went outside and happened to be filming this interesting lizard on a wall when it crept in through your mum and dad's window and…and they must have been doing it, right, but the lizard was so interesting I didn't even notice and sorry, Kev, I'm really…' As he spoke, Perry had opened the flap on the cassette and was pulling out the brown magnetic tape in great floating loops which fell on a tangled mess on the bed. 'I'm really sorry, Kev…' he repeated, unravel-ling the tape like a plastic party streamer.

Kevin shrugged. It wasn't the truth, sure, but it was kind of the truth because Perry believed it. And what did it matter? Kevin had realized, running back from the beach, that he'd also done some fairly yucky things in the past – things he didn't like to admit even to himself – and he was just lucky no one knew about them. Perry had got caught, which was bad. But…but it didn't matter now. They were mates again.

'Yeah, OK, OK, OK!' he said, keen to change the subject immediately as it started to raise the spectre of his parents...doing it, and he was fed up with thinking about that. 'Where did you see Eye Ball Paul?'

'In his limo,' replied Perry, getting all excited again. 'And Kev. He really likes our mix. He's gonna play it at the club tonight.'

'*What?*' Kevin couldn't believe his ears. Eye Ball Paul, the world's greatest living DJ (but a tiny bit of a tosser) was going to play their track – *their track*! – at Amnesia.

Mr and Mrs Patterson heard a whoop go up from the boys' room and knew instantly the lads had made up. They were both glad. It would have made the holiday unbearable if they weren't on speaking terms. Dealing with one psychotic teenager was bad enough. Coping with two of them would have been a disaster.

The boys burst out of the room grinning like a couple of mad things. 'Oh right, you're coming with us then, Perry?' asked Mr Patterson, as the lads dashed towards the door.

Perry stopped and looked at him quizzically. 'Mr Patterson?'

'For the meal?'

The boys looked at them blankly. Then a familiar shadow fell across Kevin's face, and he yanked the tie from around his neck. With a grimace of disgust and a contemptuous grunt, he threw it on the floor. Then both boys made a lunge for the front door.

'Kevin!' yelled his dad. 'Pick the tie up and give it to me, please!'

'Urggh!' moaned Kevin, throwing his arms up in the air. '*I am not your slave!*'

'Mr, Mrs...Mrs Patterson,' mumbled Perry sheepishly. The door slammed, and they were gone.

The Pattersons looked at each other.

'I liked him better with a broken heart,' said Ray, putting his arm around his wife's shoulder. She smiled at him and picked up her shawl.

Oh well, she thought, they could still go out for the meal. A quiet, uneventful night would be fun.

Quiet, and uneventful.

# chapter sixteen

Big Baz held the door open and Kevin and Perry climbed into the back of Eye Ball Paul's limousine. It was like stepping into Las Vegas. It had red leather upholstery which made the seats look like a big three-piece suite Perry had seen in World of Leather in Sidcup. There was a television, a Playstation, a drinks cabinet, a small mirror-table (the boys weren't quite sure what that was for) and more buttons and switches than Kev's mum had on her Moulinex. It was the most amazing thing either of them had ever seen, ever.

They sat facing backwards, opposite Eye Ball Paul who relaxed on the back seat with his arms out and a big grin on his face. 'Well, lads,' he said. 'You wanna see it or what?'

'See what, Eye Ball Paul?' asked Kevin, who was trying to stop Perry playing with the switches that made the seat slide backwards and forwards.

'This...' said the DJ, opening his bag and pulling out a white label vinyl record. 'Your mix.'

'Whoah!' squealed Kevin and Perry in unison.

'Can we feel it?' asked Kevin reverently. Eye Ball Paul handed over the disk to Perry, who held it gingerly with his fingers.

'It's beautiful...' cooed Perry as fondled it. He just couldn't believe it. He was a DJ. He and Kevin had *made a record*. A record that was going to be played by Eye Ball Paul, the world's greatest living DJ at *Amnesia in Ibiza*. And as if that wasn't awesome enough they were about to pick up their girlfriends in a stretch limousine with a television in it.

The car slid to a slow halt and Kevin and Perry peered out of the windows. They were at Gemma and Candice's apartment. Kevin pressed the button and the tinted glass slid effortlessly down so he could poke his head out and gaze at the balcony, where Candice and Gemma stood waiting for them. The girls, looking suitably impressed by the sight of Kevin's head appearing out of the limo, waved down at the car.

'Ladies! Comin' clubbing?' he asked suavely. They smiled and disappeared from view, emerging from the lobby moments later to find Big Baz holding the car door open for them. Feeling like royalty, they stepped in and took seats opposite the lads, either side of Eye Ball Paul.

They were beyond gorgeous. These were über-babes. Kevin and Perry could barely bring themselves to breathe. 'Alright, Candice?' croaked Kevin, in shock. Candice, who'd taken the seat in front of him, smiled and looked straight at him. This was the first time they'd made eye contact since Kev and Perry's plane had landed a few days ago.

Kev grinned and held up the record. 'We're playing our new release at the club tonight, isn't it Eye Ball Paul?' He looked to the DJ to confirm the news. It sounded too far-fetched to be real, and he really wanted Candice to know that Eye Ball Paul, the world's greatest living DJ, was going to play *their mix* at Amnesia.

Eye Ball Paul nodded. 'Yeah, that's right, boys.'

Perry took the baton. 'Yeah, it's on white label at the moment but it'll be on general release very soon. Probably.' He bounced enthusiastically in his seat, and Candice and Gemma exchanged glances. Glances that said – unmistakably – that they were seriously impressed with Kevin and Perry. This wasn't lost on Eye Ball Paul, who theatrically waved his fingers in front of his face and then placed a hand on each of the girl's thighs.

'Looks like your little minxes are very impressed, lads...' he smirked, sliding his hands further up the girls' legs.

This was not what anyone was expecting, except of course Eye Ball Paul. If it had been a boy their own age trying it on, Candice and Gemma would have floored him with a respectable right hook. But this was no ordinary mortal. This was Eye Ball Paul – world class DJ and a bloke who'd been on the front cover of *Mixmag*. What were they supposed to do? Neither had any desire to be groped by this old, *grubby* DJ – but they were in the back of his limo and maybe this was how famous people mucked about with their friends. Eye Ball Paul's hand slipped up another crucial few inches and immediately neither of the girls were left in any doubt that this was no 'mucking about'. Kevin and Perry stared in horror as Eye Ball Paul's hand disappeared up their girlfriend's skirts, and then some.

Big Baz, who'd been watching the whole thing in his rear-view mirror, slammed on the brakes, sending Gemma flying onto Perry's lap, Candice onto Kevin's lap, and Eye Ball Paul smacking hard into the glass partition between them with a satisfying slap, like a fat steak walloping onto a kitchen counter.

'Fuck!' screamed Eye Ball Paul, clutching his nose, which was bleeding a little. 'Baz, you daft bastard!'

'Sorry, Boss,' said Baz, careful not to let the DJ see how much he was grinning.

'Jesus! Why the fuck did you stop?' moaned Eye Ball Paul, reaching for a tissue and dabbing his lip.

'A little puppy ran into the road,' replied the driver.

'Shoulda flattened the little bastard,' moaned Paul.

'No!' cried the girls in unison, who were now sitting comfortably on the boys' laps and had absolutely no intention of moving next to the stinky old pervert on the back seat.

'Yeah, cos you gotta be kind to little puppies…' said Perry over his shoulder to Big Baz, even though his comment was meant exclusively for the girls' benefit.

'Yeah,' joined in Kevin. 'We love little furry animals, don't we Pel?'

This remark obviously had a profound effect on Candice, who leant over to Gemma and said: 'Only cos Kev's sensitive to the plight of all God's creatures, issit.'

'It is,' replied Gemma solemnly. 'And Perry!' With that final affirmation of approval, and unable to locate any skin that was accessible from their perch on the boys' laps, the girls gave them a kiss on their hats.

Eye Ball Paul, who'd been preoccupied with how much his nose hurt, watched in amazement as both Gemma and Candice rose slowly off the laps of their boyfriends. The boys looked embarrassed, the girls looked amazed.

He dabbed his nose with the tissue. Oh boy, this was going to be fun. He'd show the little twats who was in charge around here. Oh yes. Don't mess with the best, he thought wryly to himself. Cos the best'll just piss all over you from a very great height. Large.

Mr and Mrs Patterson strolled hand in hand up the street, the sea breeze wafting warm air around them amid the hubbub of the lively street life, swirling them with layered smells of food, drink and smoke. They'd taken to going for an early evening walk after a late afternoon siesta (Ray's rather shy euphemism for their increasingly enjoyable bouts of afternoon sex) and as they neared the end of the vacation they wanted to explore some of the livelier parts of town.

'It's been a fantastic holiday, love,' said Ray smiling down at his wife. 'Just what we needed.' And he was right. It *was* just what they needed. A break from the routine. A chance to rediscover each other. An opportunity to bring the sparkle back into their lives. After years of drudgery and aggro with Kevin, it was surprising to think that a holiday with him would actually solve the problem. In reality, of course, the 'problem' of Kevin hadn't been solved at all. Instead, they'd simply discovered how to stop his selfishness upsetting them: be selfish themselves. And that's what they'd done. Be selfish. Whenever they wanted. Wherever they wanted.

'Yes, we needed to give the boys a break,' said Mrs Patterson. 'Thanks for doing that, Ray.'

'Thanks to you,' he said genuinely. 'I feel liberated. Truly liberated. They're not bad lads really.' As he spoke, they rounded a corner and found themselves outside an enormous building with lights all over the front. Amnesia, it said in big letters across the top of the entrance. It reminded Mr Patterson of something he'd heard Kevin talk with Perry about before they left. 'Isn't that one of those disco places Kevin and Perry go to?' he asked, nodding at the club. As he spoke he saw two familiar figures step out of a limousine by the front entrance with two girls on their arms. 'And look,' he added, pointing across the road. 'Isn't that them?' They stared at the boys and, sure enough, it was Kevin and Perry. 'Let's go in,' said Ray, suddenly feeling very dangerous indeed.

'Don't be silly!'

'They'll never see us with all these people. It'll be an experience. Aren't you curious?' He looked at his wife and saw a flicker in her eyes, the same flicker that was there twenty years ago when they stole her dad's car that summer night and made love in the back seat while parked round the side of the local church. Or when they'd just finished college and she suggested they take all their savings and go to Gatwick, and jump on the first plane out they could afford. They'd ended up washing dishes in a restaurant in Madrid to buy their tickets back.

She grinned. Why not? It *would* be an experience. 'Oh go on then...' she said, straightening her dress. What a blast...

'This is it Pel,' said Kevin, looking up to the entrance and clutching the white label to his chest. And this *was* it. That same feeling he'd had at home when he thought he couldn't get to Ibiza. That same feeling of destiny. Of being supposed to be here, like all moments had led up to this.

'Kev?' said Perry, breaking his train of thought.

'Yeah?'

'Let's mash it up, Kev. Large.'

'Yeah,' smirked Kevin. 'Large!'

Eye Ball Paul swept past them and they suddenly realized they had the records to bring in. They started to go round the back of the car when Baz waved them away. 'Don't worry, lads,' he said, lifting two big aluminium cases onto the pavement. 'I'll manage. This is your night.'

They gave Baz a big thumbs-up, and with Candice and Gemma on their arms, marched into the entrance. Eye Ball Paul must obviously have put the word out because all the bouncers stepped to one side and they floated into the club on a cushion of good wishes.

They followed Eye Ball Paul through a series of passages and doors until they emerged into the throbbing, thumping heat of the club, high up in the DJ's booth. Kev and Perry gawped at the set-up. They'd never seen so many turntables before. It obviously worked much the same way as their gear at home – mixers for each of the feeds, digital effects decks, rhythm boxes and all the rest of the stuff a good DJ needs – but it was still pretty impressive. And what an awesome position for the booth. There wasn't an inch of the club they couldn't see. Behind them, an enormous video screen played computer-generated graphics in time to the music, whilst huge gantries of lights and lasers swung down from the roof to kick off different beats, building the crowd up or letting them down slowly in a breathtaking display of smoke, light and music.

Kev looked around in amazement. This was power. This was *sex*. This was…words failed him. If you wanted to get off on it, this was what being a DJ was all about. Forget the choons. It was about being in control of these people, making them do whatever you wanted.

He looked at Eye Ball Paul and it was like a thick fog suddenly cleared in front of him. No wonder Eye Ball Paul was such a twat. And he *was* a twat, no doubt about it. This was what he lived for. Being in charge, being a dickhead control-freak. It had nothing to do with making good music, making people feel good about themselves, giving them something to hum in their head on the way to the beach in the morning. It was about making them do what you wanted them to do. It wasn't being cool, it was being fascist.

Kevin felt confused, exhilarated, grown-up.

145

He watched the DJ grab the mike, and take charge of the beats on the tables. 'Are you on a good one?' he shouted, soaking up the adoration. The crowd erupted, waving at Paul and generally letting him know how pleased they were that he was now in charge. 'Are you 'avin it large?' shouted Eye Ball Paul and this time the response was even bigger. The DJ turned to Kev and Pel. 'With me on the decks got two new spars! Tell 'em your names compadres!'

Kev leant into the microphone. 'Er...hello, I'm Kevin.' He handed the mike to Perry.

'DJ Mixmaster Prince Perr. E. of the Supersonic Decks. Keeping it real!' They saluted the crowd – Kevin a bit peeved Perry had out-cooled him – and watched in awe as Eye Ball Paul held up their white label disc.

'You heard it here first. "Oooh Ray Ibiza!"' He grinned, flipped the disc, then lined it up on the turntable, ready to go.


Mr and Mrs Patterson thought they'd been transported to the middle of the Gulf War, or maybe gone back in time and ended up on the Western Front during the Battle of the Somme. The noise was unbelievable. Truly, and very literally, breathtaking. The bass was so tangible Mr Patterson could feel his chest clench with every skull-crushing, ear-splitting beat of the music. Well, he thought it was music. It might have been the noise from some incredibly inefficient manufacturing plant – one with rows of steel hammers, panel beaters and thudding, rivet-melting metallic mallets pounding away. And over the sound of clanging girders and nearby exploding mortar fire was the insistent electronic shrill of repetitive and insistent car alarms, the persistent bleeping of video games and reversing lorries. It was dreadful. Truly, awfully, mind-numbingly horrid.

But despite all this, the noise, the heat, the crush, there was a kind of hypnotic, communal trance-like state it induced – a powerful group hypnosis that enveloped the whole crowd and infused the event with a sense of togetherness that Ray thought probably hadn't been witnessed since the Hitler Youth rallies. It was, like he'd said outside, an experience. Not one he'd want to repeat, but it *was* an experience.

There was a tug at his sleeve and he turned to his wife, who was pointing somewhere above their heads. They'd given up trying to converse since they'd got in, and had resorted to ad hoc hand signals and amateur semaphore. He looked up into the lights, where there was some kind of control booth, and to his shock he saw Kevin and Perry waving to the crowd. Some gangly chap with the microphone introduced them and the crowd erupted into cheers. The boys both said something into the microphone (which in all honesty they couldn't really understand) and then the other bloke – the DJ probably – held a record above his head.

'IT'S THEIR RECORD!' screamed Mrs Patterson into Ray's ear.

'WHAT?'

'IT'S THEIR RECORD. KEVIN AND PERRY. HE'S GOING TO PLAY *THEIR RECORD*!'

Ray frowned, wondering what on earth she was talking about. And then it dawned on him. *It was their record!* All that rubbish about wanting to be a DJ might actually be true. Kevin and Perry had – in Ray's old rock 'n' roll parlance – got themselves a gig. He turned to Mrs Patterson and smiled. Kevin had got a gig.

Blimey!

The beat changed to something a bit less...'industrial', and the crowd cheered. Whatever it was, they seemed to like it. Then a little catchy bit started to come in over the top of the beat, and then a woman's voice crying 'Oooh Ray... Ooohhh Ray'.

The video screen above the DJ's booth switched from abstract computer graphics to a video image. A picture of two people having sex.

– Oooh Ray, Ohhh Ray

*Sex in an apartment room*

– Oooh Ray, Ooohhh Ray

*Their apartment room*

– Oooh Ray, Ohhh Ray

*Them having sex in their apartment*

– Oooh Ray, Ohhh Ray

*Mrs Patterson writhing on top of Mr Patterson*

– Oooh Ray, Ohhh Ray

*On the video screen*

– Ooh Ray, Oooohhhh Ray

Mr Patterson felt his bowels loosen and a dry, acid lump lodged in his throat. His hand fumbled at his side and he took hold of his wife's fingers, holding them tight in case she ran off. He turned and looked at her ashen upturned face as she stared at the video screen. This was a video of them having sex. Intimate, private, personal sex. On a video screen. In front of about a thousand people. Very, very loudly.

The music changed again and Ray recognized Kevin and Perry's voices singing 'Big Girl! Big Girl!' – a refrain which he'd asked Kevin to turn down more times than he cared to remember. Now things were getting really surreal. He had absolutely no idea what was going on. But whatever it was, he'd never felt more humiliated than he did right now.

The moment Kev heard the familiar start to 'Big Girl! Big Girl!' he knew Eye Ball Paul wasn't stitching them up. This was their song – almost identical to the mix they'd left on the demo tape – and now it was being played at Amnesia. Judging by the way the crowd were bouncing up and down, it seemed to be going down quite well. On the dance floor he could see Candice and Gemma, who gave the boys a quick wave and flashed them a smile.

But then the video screen flashed into life, and there, two metres high, three metres wide and suspended over the clubbiest, raviest crowd in Ibiza, were his parents having sex. 'Ooohhh Ray...' went a new chorus that Eye Ball Paul had mixed into their choon. Kevin recoiled as if he'd been slapped. His parents! Having sex! All the old horrors returned, but this time with an even greater grip of embarrassment. Kev looked down at the crowd, expecting them to be as revolted and appalled as he was. But instead, they seemed to be cheering. Cheering the song. Their song! What was going on?

Then the picture changed and Kevin found himself looking up at his own enormous face leering into the crowd. 'Candice...' he boomed from the sound system. 'Suck my candy...!'

*Oh flippity flip flip. The tape! That night they went out recording!*

The image changed again, and this time it was Perry's enormous mug that leered down at the crowd. 'Gemma... Gemma... Gemma,' he moaned. 'Lick my love plank, Gemma. Lick!'

The boys looked at each other in utter terror. Embarrassed was a gross understatement of how they were feeling at this moment. They'd get chucked now, sure as anything, and they'd deserve it. They both peered over the edge of the DJ's booth to see if they could find Candice and Gemma. The girls were there in the middle of the dance floor, jumping up and down and screaming. That was it, then. They were dumped.

'We're famous...' yelled the girls, laughing. 'WE'RE FAMOUS!' The girls hugged and waved up at the boys. 'We love ya!' they screamed.

By now the crowd had come alive like never before at Amnesia. The combination of the video and the music had them bouncing up and down and giving it as large as it had ever been given. The place was going mental.

'All I wanna do is...do it!' came Kevin's voice over the track.

'Ooohhh Ray, Ooohhh Ray' went Mrs Patterson's voice immediately afterwards.

'That's enough of that shit,' came Eye Ball Paul's petulant voice, followed by the angry skid of the needle being plucked from the record. The crowd roared in disappointment as a pissed-off looking Eye Ball Paul yanked Kevin and Perry's track off the turntable and stuck another on.

This wasn't what he was expecting at all. He wanted the boys to get humiliated. Embarrassed. Chucked. Booed at.

But now the only booing was directed at him.

'Put it back on!' came a few shouts from the floor.

'Get off!'

'More!'

'Nobody likes you anymore!'

Eye Ball Paul's beat kicked in, but no one was dancing. An empty water bottle whizzed past his head and the booing increased.

'Dance, you scumbags!' shouted the DJ, but no one moved. Instead, the crowd started chanting.

'Oooh Ray, Oooh Ray!' they yelled. The boys could not believe what was happening. First the video, now this. Did this lot actually want *their* track instead of Eye Ball Paul's? Eye Ball Paul seemed to think so, because he grabbed their white label and held it above his head.

'You want a piece of this shit?' he yelled, spittle flying from his mouth in an ugly, ropy spray. 'You can each have a little bit of it!' He brought the record crashing down towards the deck but just before it made contact a big, beefy hand appeared out of nowhere and stopped it in mid-air.

'Don't do that, boss,' said Big Baz coolly.

'What the fuck…?' stammered Eye Ball Paul.

'I think they want to hear it again.' Baz yanked the record out of the DJ's hand.

'You're fired!' screamed Eye Ball Paul. Big Baz smiled. A smile Eye Ball Paul had never seen before. A smile full of self-confidence. Purpose. And intense dislike.

'I should have done this ages ago.'

'What?' spluttered Eye Ball Paul, now very unsettled. As he spoke, Big Baz's fist came powering out of nowhere and landed on the DJ's chin with a satisfying snapping sound. The force of the punch clean lifted Eye Ball Paul off the floor, over the top of the turntables, where he flew gracelessly through the air and landed on his back in the middle of the dance floor, dazed and winded. The crowd erupted into cheers, swarmed to fill the gap left by Eye Ball Paul's prostrate gasping figure, and began chanting again for the boys.

Big Baz handed them the record. 'It's all yours, lads…'

Candice and Gemma looked on adoringly from the dance floor as Perry took the record and put it on the turntable. He looked at Kev, they grabbed the mikes, and launched into their first ever live gig at Amnesia.

The first of many.


'Beautiful, innit,' said Kev, lying on the sand and watching the sun creep above the horizon in a blaze of vibrant gold.

'Like you, issit,' replied Candice, who had her head on Kevin's chest and was hugging him tight.

'It is,' sniggered Kevin, feeling like he owned the world. He'd lost his virginity. Not just lost his virginity, but done it three times, to the loveliest girl in the whole world. His girlfriend Candice! It all seemed so unreal. The club. The snogging. *The sex.*

'Is that you shagging on the record?' whispered Candice into his ear.

'Yeah, might be…' said Kevin, trying to sound casual and mysterious, hoping Candice might think he was a monsta rinsin' love machine who'd done it lots.

'Who's the bird?' asked Candice.

'My mum…' replied Kevin, without thinking. Candice propped herself up and looked at him quizzically. Kevin realized what he'd said and tried to backtrack. 'Oh! No… I mean. It's not me! I'd never done it before and… and…' He gave up, embarrassed that he'd had to mention his mum, and even more embarrassed about admitting to not having had sex before.

'Were you a virgin?' she asked, smiling.

'Er…no,' said Kev unconvincingly. Candice smiled. She didn't believe him, of course not. Boys would never admit to being a virgin, even when everyone knew they were.

'So was I,' she said, lying back down. Kevin stroked her hair, and they started kissing again. Big fruity kisses.

On the other side of the sand dune, Perry kissed Gemma's cheek and nestled into her neck. 'I love you…' he whispered.

'Yeah, cos me too,' she said sweetly. 'Cos you're cute and sexily attentive to a girl's needs. And give it to 'er large.' Perry grinned. Give it to her large. That was brilliant! He heard a noise from behind him and sat up.

'Kev?' he hissed.

'Yeah,' came a voice from behind the sand dune.

'Have you done it?'

There was a momentary pause as Kevin struggled with answering the question in front of Candice. 'Er... yeah,' he said eventually.

'So've I!' said Perry. 'Did you give it to Candice large?' Over on the other side of the dune Kevin looked imploringly at Candice, who couldn't quite believe what Perry was asking. She smiled at Kev and shrugged.

'I think so,' said Kevin sheepishly, as Candice climbed on top of him and started snogging fiercely. One thing was certain.

He wasn't a virgin anymore.

Kev grabbed Candice and rolled over in the sand.

One more time wouldn't do any harm.

# chapter seventeen

Sharon stood with her mates in the queue waiting to get Kev and Pel's autographs. The shop was heaving and the two hit DJs had been signing records since the store opened at eight that morning. Their song 'Big Girl!' had been an enormous hit since taking the Ibiza club scene by storm during the summer and now the boys were the hottest act on the scene.

Sharon stepped up to the table and handed the boys her record. She smiled at them and Kev signed the CD with an enormously flamboyant signature which covered half the disk in curly swirls and twisty loops. Sharon thought it was very cool. Without actually looking Kevin in the eye she mumbled her thanks and, with a gaggle of mates around her, scuttled off to the other side of the record store.

Stacey, her best friend, gathered the group of girls together. 'Ere,' she said. 'I told you it was true, Sharon shagged 'im before 'e was famous, didn't ya Sharon?'

'That's right,' said Sharon preening herself slightly. 'It was at this party and we did it all night. Then we went to one of his gigs togevver. At the Arndale. It was brilliant.'

The girls cooed. That was so cool. Kevin was so cool. And Perry. Well, 'e was well cute, wasn't 'e? They

154

giggled to themselves as they walked out of the store, right past a second record shop next door. In the window sat a forlorn, depressed figure at an empty table, a big bin of CDs next to him labelled 'Has Beens At Half Price' and 'Last Year's Losers'. He watched as the girls floated disinterestedly past the store without so much as looking at him and he groaned. Something was going on nearby which was why no one had come in yet to his record signing. What a pisser.

He needed booze. That would make it better.

He reached under the table and grabbed the bottle of Stolly he kept for emergencies, tipped back his head and poured a generous serving over his open eye.

'Ahhhhhhh… TWAT!' he screamed loudly, as the vodka kicked in and burned his face. 'FUCKIN' TWATS!!!'

No one heard him. There was too much going on next door.

Ernest Buchan looked up from his mowing in order to try and track down the source of the strange noises he was hearing. He turned off the mower and allowed the engine to slow to a stutter, then craned his head in the direction of the sound. It was coming from the Patterson's next door. He looked over to their house, and sure enough, that was where the commotion was coming from.

He tutted. They used to be such a nice family — except that layabout son of theirs. And now look what had happened. First the boy turns into some sort of pop star or DJ or something, with that lumpen twit, Perry. And if that wasn't bad enough, with a constant stream of teenage girls hanging around asking for their autographs, his parents have to get all famous with that disgusting book of theirs. What was it called…*Better*

155

*Mid-Marriage Sex* or something similar. It was sickening, people carrying on like that. He'd had a look at it in the bookstore in town the other day and it was filthy. Talking about massages and hot oils and bubble baths and handcuffs and silk sheets and...and... He shuddered. It was all too grim. Thank goodness he and Mary didn't indulge in such mucky shenanigans. That's how you got children, that was, and who wanted them, hey?

He looked over to the house where two brand new scooters sat in the drive with the number plates DJ PEL and DJ KEV – whatever that was supposed to mean. And as for that new Jag the Pattersons had got themselves. OOH RAY was the silly personalized number plate on that one and Ernest Buchan had a good idea what *that* referred to.

The noises got louder and he tried to place them. From one corner of the house it sounded like someone was moaning 'Ooh Candice'. From somewhere else he could hear 'Ooh Perry' and 'Ooh Gemma' all mixed in together and then, from round the back, 'Ooh Ray' and what sounded suspiciously like 'Oooh Barbarella'.

A shiver ran up his spine. It was like living next door to a bloody bordello.

He yanked the chain on the mower and it spluttered into life, then pushed it so as to make sure he'd got the lines in the grass perfectly straight. Wouldn't do to miss a bit.

He glanced over at the house again.

Bloody Pattersons. Weirdos, every last one of them.